A Bathory Universe Novel

Time OF THE *Ancients*

SPECIAL EDITION

Get bitten!

NSFW EDITION

THE BORN VAMPIRE SERIES BOOK SIX

ELIZABETH DUNLAP

INTRODUCTION

Warning: For Adult Audiences 18+. Language and actions may be deemed offensive to some. Sexually explicit content. M/F, M/M/F/M

OTHER BOOKS BY ELIZABETH DUNLAP

Born Vampire Series: Ya Edition (Completed)

Knight of the Hunted (1)

Child of the Outcast (2)

War of the Chosen (3)

Bite of the Fallen (4)

Rise of the Monsters (5)

Time of the Ancients (6)

Born Vampire Series: NSFW Edition (Completed)

Knight of the Hunted (1)

Child of the Outcast (2)

War of the Chosen (3)

Bite of the Fallen (4)

Rise of the Monsters (5)

Time of the Ancients (6)

Born Vampire Short Stories

Tales of the Favored: Arthur's Tale (3.5)

Affairs of the Immortal: The Sinful Affair (4.4)

Affairs of the Immortal: The Knight and Arthur Affair (4.5)

Affairs of the Immortal: The Valentine's Day Affair (6.5)

Dedicated to my gal group, who kept insisting this series was reverse harem even though it wasn't at first.
Balthazar wins. The end.

THE MAGIC BEGINS

J woke up in a tangle of limbs. With several legs over mine, two arms slung across my stomach, and someone's face planted against my hair, it was hard to tell where they ended and I began. Carefully, I extracted myself from my two lovers' embrace and slid off the end of our big bed, only to turn around and see they had already filled my empty space by snuggling with each other. Knight sleepily raised his head and kissed Arthur's lips, then he curled up closer to the icy warrior who held him close like he was his precious teddy bear.

Yeah. That was happening now.

One day I'd come home from visiting my parents only to find Arthur passionately kissing my husband while jacking him off, and it made for some very hot sex afterwards, no complaints. Now they were bonded mates in addition to being my mates, and our little ménage trio was doing well. I'll admit that seeing them making out while still in a sleepy haze was a major turn on, but I had to get up and make sure breakfast was ready by the time the kids were up.

"Don't fuck without me," I threw over my shoulder as I bent to our communal chest of drawers so I could get dressed for the day. Pulling some clothes and my jewelry from a drawer, I heard some lazy protests before heavy moaning filled the air and I turned back to see my lovers making out still with their hands on each other's hard erections. My dress and necklace fell to the floor, and I was very glad I was already naked. "Or this is good too."

Knight sat up, throwing me a devilish grin that sent shivers all over my body, and he knelt in front of Arthur before sliding his hard cock inside the vampire so hard it brought a long drawn out groan from Arthur's lips. The view of Knight's smooth, round ass from where I was standing as he started thrusting in and out of our lover was too much for me to handle. I eagerly climbed back onto the bed and ran my hand up and down his buttocks, smacking one cheek and then the other, making him moan and throw his head back.

"Come here," Arthur said breathlessly, tugging at my knee. I crawled over to him, squealing when Knight returned the favor and smacked my ass back. Arthur was gripping the sheets already from the intensity of my husband's fucking, but he carefully guided me to the spot he wanted, where my dripping slit was right over his face. I gripped the headboard and jerked upright at the first tease of his tongue along my folds. His rough hands held me in place so I couldn't escape the ruthless tongue lashing I was about to receive, even if I got too sensitive for it. He knew exactly what I liked.

Arthur lowered me onto his tongue and immediately suckled my clitoris into his mouth, rolling his tongue across it until I was gasping against the headboard, almost unsure if I could still hold myself up before he was finished with me. He brought a hand up and slid two fingers inside my pussy, fucking me in and out in time with his mouth. A low guttural groan escaped my lips as I grew slightly sensitive from his intensity and I tried to move away if only for a second.

A firm hand landed on my head, holding me in place by a chunk of my hair, pressing my cheek into the wall behind our bed. "Don't even think about moving, Lis," Knight commanded, his voice husky and slightly out of breath from his ravenous fucking. "Make her come, Arthur. She can't get away." Knight had taken a tip from our lover, becoming more assertive with me sexually, and yes, it was the hottest thing ever. He was also right, I was completely pinned between them, unable to move with Knight's hand firmly holding my head and Arthur's arm cupped around my waist so I couldn't lift my hips. Knowing I was so helpless drove me absolutely wild, making it no surprise I was about to climax.

Arthur pushed into both our heads since we were all connected now through my psychic abilities. *She's tightening up on my fingers, she really can't resist us holding her in place. We should definitely tie her up again.* I moaned from the memory of the last time they'd tied me up. Arthur tied me to a kitchen chair, legs spread, breasts bare, so I could watch him fuck Knight in the ass until he came all over my naked body. Then Arthur pulled my hips forward and fucked my ass in the chair, not letting me orgasm until I begged for him to tie me up more often. Then he allowed Knight to flick my clit once, sending me careening off into the abyss of a climax so intense I almost passed out.

"That was a good memory," Knight purred, the sound of his balls hitting Arthur's ass the only sound I could hear over my own moans. I'd accidentally sent both of them a replay of that day, and the slight humiliation sent an erotic pulse through me, shoving me over the edge until I was coming on Arthur's tongue over and over, unable to even move my head beyond sagging against the headboard. "Don't stop, keep licking her."

Hazy, I was about to ask what he was doing when I felt Knight probing my ass and sliding his cock inside me, with the hand on my head not slacking for one second. His other hand reached around and grasped one of my breasts, flicking the nipple until I gasped and bucked my hips because the sensations were too intense. Arthur's tongue on my clit, his fingers in my pussy, and Knight's cock moving in and out of my ass. My tired body didn't know whether to shy away or beg for more. Either way, the option was no longer mine because they had me and they would do whatever they wanted to me. And gods, I loved it.

Knight's hot breath fluttered over my neck and he pulled me away from the wall until I was flush against his back and he was holding me in place again as he fucked away at my ass. God, he was so good at this. He was tireless, even when he went at a blinding pace and thrust so hard it almost hurt. The effect on me though was palpable, making my pussy gush around Arthur's fingers and my body awash with pleasure.

Without even realizing, I hit that sweet spot and started babbling out from the haze I was in. "Fuck, fuck me harder. I need to come again."

Greedy, Arthur sent to me, almost chuckling against my clitoris.

In response, Knight started pulling me away from Arthur's mouth and I gripped the headboard to stop him. "No, no! I want to come." But Knight wasn't listening, he pulled me down Arthur's body so I was poised above Arthur's still erect penis and I was lowered onto it until they were both inside me, filling me to the brim. I was still close enough to a climax that I could hardly think, but I gripped Arthur's arms when he sat up and they both started a rhythm of fucking me in and out, making it impossible for me to go back. Groans bubbled from my throat and Knight pulled at my hair again until I was immobile against him, and he made sure to capture my hands so I couldn't rub myself to make this happen any faster.

Ass.

"Connect us," Knight ordered into my ear, biting at the lobe slightly. As soon as I did, their mutual sensations filled me, making me so overwhelmed I felt like I was floating over the room. Knight was holding himself off so much, he could hardly stand it, seeing me so overcome was about to make him lose it. Arthur was enjoying the view of both of his lovers together and the sight was having the same effect on him, and especially after being nicely fucked before me, he was dangerously close to the edge. I couldn't take it, I started coming in a never ending wave that swept them along with me until I literally passed out from the pleasure.

When I woke up for the second time that morning, I was still entwined with various limbs, only this time we were a sweaty heap that was completely drained for the rest of the century. Grunting, I shoved a leg off of my ribcage and was swept into a cuddle spoon before I could react. Knight clutched me to him, nuzzling my naked ass into the crook of his body where we fit perfectly together. Arthur was on my other side, pushing himself against my breasts and planting soft kisses along my cheek and lips.

"Balthazar is coming over," I got out in-between kisses.

"Mmm," Arthur buzzed against my lips. "He can watch."

That brought me reeling back so I could catch the look on his face, just to be sure he was in fact joking. "That's not funny, babe."

"S'not like he's never seen you naked," Knight noted sleepily against my bare shoulder. "Trust me, he's got a hard-on for you still."

I wiggled out of their arms because the conversation was going somewhere I wasn't sure I liked. "Okay, ha ha. Don't tease me. Yes, we fucked and it was amazing. That was sixty-seven years ago. Also we're not talking about this," I emphasized after I picked my dress up from the floor. I threw it over my head and flipped my curls out in a huff, not bothering with my necklace that I put on top of the dresser.

"How long did it take you to accept your feelings for Arthur," my husband said dryly, giving me a knowing look.

Why? Why did I have to end up with two men who ganged up on me at every turn, bringing out the painful things I tried to avoid?

My scowl in his direction stayed as I pulled out some underwear and slipped it on under my dress. "This is not the same thing, Knight. It has never been the same thing, and it will never be the same thing." After walking to the door and turning back, my eyes landed on Arthur's icy face and he was giving me that look that meant he thought I was wrong. "No, you keep that look to yourself. You're wrong. You're both wrong. I love you both, but stick it up your ass."

That was my send-off to their naked butts as I shut the bedroom door behind me.

Damn men and their meddling therapy sessions. I loved the absolute piss out of them, but *gods*, why would they say something like that? They had no idea what they were talking about. I knew my head and my heart.

"Lisbeth, good morning," Balthazar said, suddenly in front of me.

"God, stop that!" I waved my hand at him, somehow unable to look him in the eye, and walked through the den to the dining room where little nine year old Gwen sat at the table drawing a picture. I kissed the top of her dark head on my way to the kitchen where I got out several pots to make breakfast in. Balthazar rounded the corner in between the dining room and kitchen, making me jump again. "Fuck, it's like you've gained the ability to be incorporeal again. God forbid," I said dryly with a laugh, but he was meeting my awkward look with a curious expression. I cleared my throat and opened the fridge door, blocking him from my view so I could pick up our bowl of eggs.

God damn it.

"You smell of love," he said from behind the door, and I closed it with a whoosh of air to look up at him.

"And you smell like lilacs." Fuck, my burns were weak. I wrinkled my nose in disgust at myself and turned to the stove. "So, where's George? The guy that lives at the abandoned movie theater?" I didn't have to specify who I was talking about because he was our only neighbor named George. Balthazar had negotiated blood rations with the man and they'd become friends along the way.

As I started prepping the meal, I realized our egg bowl only had one egg inside it because I'd been too distracted to notice. Eager for an excuse to get away from my oldest friend, I reached under the counter for our egg basket and popped up with a smile. "I need to go gather eggs. I'll be back in two shakes of a lamb's tail."

I rushed outside the kitchen through the back door and wiped a stray curl from my now sweaty forehead. *What was wrong with me?* I'd never thought of Balthazar romantically since the night I conceived Kitty after mindless fucking that had me drooling like a sex crazed idiot, but was that because I had no feelings for him, or because I'd very soon afterwards had my affections spoken for with someone else?

Fuck, feelings were the worst.

I trod along the field outside our house to the chicken coop Knight and Arthur built when we came here over ten years ago. After building it, they spent the better part of a month tracking down wild chickens to fill it with so we could have fresh eggs. The chickens clucked and fluttered around my bare feet when I opened the gate and shut it behind me. Wading through a large group of the birds, I lifted the hen house roof and started reaching inside to gather the eggs from the nests. Several brooding hens were actually sitting on theirs so I gently stuck my fingers under their feathers to pull out the eggs they'd laid. One bright red hen pecked my hand in protest, but I pat her head anyway and shut the roof after I was done.

A rooster crowed at me when I walked past him while something startled the birds on the other side of the coop. My ears hadn't caught the sound with my distracted mood, and now that I used my senses, I could feel a human nearby. I smelled her blood, fresh and crisp. The chickens flew at me when I rushed to exit the coop, but they didn't escape like they'd planned to. I set the egg basket down in the grass and ran towards the smell of fresh blood.

Not far away from the coop stood a large oak tree with a corpse underneath it. No, not a corpse. Her pulse was still thrumming rapidly in her veins, but it was weak. Far too weak. She resembled my mother's appearance when we'd first met, with a ratty, torn black dress and matted, dirty hair. Who was this woman?

I bent to help her up and she wheezed out a breath that sounded eerily like she had a punctured lung. "Let me help you," I assured her soothingly as I helped prop her up against the tree trunk. The blood I was smelling came from a wound in her side, and I knew it was one she would not survive.

"Li—" she broke off and coughed in a fit that blew spurts of blood onto her hand. I picked her up and carried her from the tree to our water pump to get her a glass of water. She took it gratefully and drank deeply of the cool liquid. "Lisbeth," she said hoarsely, looking up at me.

I was taken aback that this creature knew my name. "You know me?" I couldn't recall knowing anyone that looked like her. Maybe her face was too dirty to tell properly. I wet the corner of my dress to wipe at her filthy cheeks to see if I could clean her up enough to jog my memory.

"No," she protested, pushing my hands away. "There's no time. If I die first, nothing will matter."

"Lisbeth?" Knight's voice came from the back door behind me. "Who is that?"

The woman took my hand and clutched it to her chest. "I'm Selene Halace. I was a professor at Highborn Academy before the sharks came." Highborn? I'd never heard of it. Was it a prep school? "Here, take this. It will guide you to Highborn when you get back." She pressed a compass necklace into my hands and coughed again with more blood appearing on her dress and chin. "I've been looking for you for so long. If you can't help us, then no one can."

"I'm going to take you inside, one of my husbands is a doctor." I tried to stand but she tugged me back down again.

"No, you don't understand. I'm not going to survive this either way. I'm sorry that what I have to do will come at such a price. If there were any way I could prevent that, know that I would do it."

Even though she wasn't making sense, I'd become engrossed in her words as a sick feeling settled in my stomach. "What price? What am I doing that involves a sacrifice?" I tried brushing some of her hair back from her face and felt her scorching hot forehead.

"You have to save the world again. You have to prevent Alistair from destroying the humans, and the only way you can is if I send you back to before the war happened." Her words were absurd, and I could barely form a thought to argue them with my head starting to spin in confusion. "I'm the last witch alive, and if I'm gone, there will be no one guarding the portal. If the portal opens, the world will be destroyed again, and this time, there will be no going back."

I blinked and a tear dropped from my eyelashes. Why was I crying? "You said something about a price? And what do you mean by send me back?"

"You'll never see this version of your family again. Your children. Your husbands. You can get them back, but they won't be the same."

In a rush, I straightened and turned as if the world had slowed to a crawl, facing the house where Gwen stood next to Knight and Arthur. Even with my brain trying to wrap itself around this, I reached out to them just as Selene shot her hand out to grasp my ankle. An electric shot went up my leg and I sprang away from her only for her body to fall dead on the ground.

"Mommy!" Gwen cried out to me, running towards me from the steps of the porch with Knight behind her. My legs were stuck to the earth, I couldn't move. My hand reached to them, but before they could get to me, everything disappeared into a flood of black.

2

BLOOD AND COFFEE

J woke up to the scent of blood in my room. Blood and coffee.

Wait. No. I've done this before.

I shot up from my bed—when was I in bed... oh god. All around me was a room I hadn't seen in over fifty years. The cream walls, the vanilla carpet, the golden comforter.

And to my side was...

A shirtless Cameron looked up from his phone, a grin on his perfect, beautiful face. "Sorry, you were shouting in your slee—" I cut him off, launching myself off the bed and into his arms where our combined weight broke the chair he was sitting on.

"I love you, I love you, I love you," I repeated, kissing him all over his face with one chaste kiss to his lips before I hugged him to my body so tightly he grunted in pain.

Cameron was back. He wasn't dead anymore. He wasn't a smoking corpse in the city that held me captive for years with that fucking bastard Hendrix. And the fact that Cameron was here meant...

Selene had sent me back in time. Back to the day before my life had changed forever.

Tomorrow Simon would cross the vampire border, and if I wasn't there to protect him, someone else might see him and do the unspeakable thing that I couldn't do: kill a child. It would only make sense that someone else had been there, because how else had the Order found out?

"Why are you kissing me? That's so gross, stop it!" I hugged him through his protests until he hung limp against me. A knock sounded at the front door of the suite and my memories of this day flipped out like file folders, running over my eyes until I was efficiently refreshed on everything.

I had no time to feel the whiplash of time travel. My first action had to be finding the Highborn school thing. Looking down, I saw the compass around my neck with the needle pointing steadily right out my window. I had to get my children and my husbands back. Nothing else mattered.

"That'll be Othello," Cameron smarted in annoyance. Ahh shit, I'd have to go through the motions of this day. Goddd, I did not want to do this. I wanted to leave immediately and get my life back from that fucking *witch*.

"Yes, that man does not know when to quit," I said before I could stop myself, popping a hand over my mouth as

TIME OF THE ANCIENTS NSFW SPECIAL EDITION

Cameron raised a curious eyebrow at me. I'd said exactly what he was going to say.

"Yeah. That. Be sure to let him down easy this time." He helped extricate us both from the broken chair and sat down on the edge of my bed to continue with his game, leaving me to deal with another face I hadn't seen in many years. A robe waited for me on the handle of my bathroom door and I put it on while heading towards the front door, steeling myself for this moment with gritted teeth.

I opened the heavy door and came face to face with my ancient nemesis, the leader of my Order, Othello, who was holding a bouquet of roses to offset his deathly pale face. God, he was as gross looking as I remembered. I pasted on a smile and leaned against my doorway, making sure to keep the door as closed as possible so he wouldn't see Cameron when he came from my room in about ten seconds.

"Those for me?"

Othello brightened like a light, my sudden enthusiasm very different from how I used to treat him back in that day, and he chimed in with his thick British butler accent. "Yes, of course! Good morning, Lisbeth."

"Morning, boss." Ahh, this was a good day. I wasn't in charge of the entire fucking race of vampires yet. Maybe I never would be now. Yay me.

Othello's vacant eyes eagerly followed my movements as I marveled at the beautiful flowers in his hands. It had been so long since I'd seen roses as lovely as the ones he'd brought me. "Yes, yes. It's almost time for the meeting. It'll be in the drawing-room."

We both said his last line simultaneously.

"The bigger one."

I finger gunned him and winked. "Totes. Got it, boss man. However, I kind of have a date today. I'm busy."

He was taken aback, as if it hadn't occurred to him that I'd even consider looking for someone else to fill my bed. He covered the emotion quickly, adjusting his jacket and cravat before slicking down his greasy hair in one movement. "We have the turning, Lisbeth. This is your role here; I won't have you shirking your responsibilities."

I clicked my tongue and shrugged, rolling my eyes towards the ceiling. "I'd agree with you, but this is one hot piece of ass we're talking about. I can't just *not go*. Can we re-schedule to tomorrow?" Not that I was planning on being there the next day, but it wasn't like I had a solid plan yet.

Othello looked like I'd just flashed him my boobs, completely flabbergasted to silence that was only broken by partial words as he tried to form a response. "You... This isn't..."

"I feel ya, boss man," I comforted, throwing a hand out to pat him on his jacketed shoulder. "But if you'll recall, I've never asked for anything ever. Can't I get just one little bitty tiny pass?" I held out two fingers to make a tiny space between them and stuck out my bottom lip. God, I was flirting with the ugliest guy in the world.

He was flustered for a few more seconds before he

adjusted his jacket again and straightened his spine. "Okay, we will postpone the turning one day. Only one."

"Awesome! High five!" I held out a hand and Othello stared at it like it had poison thorns. Shit. I wasn't acting like old me at all. This was me after over sixty years of being married to Knight.

Fuck. He wasn't with me yet. The memory he was out there not even knowing who I was did not sit well with me. I remembered the look on his face before I'd disappeared, and the look on Gwen's face as she ran towards me with fear all over her beautiful little features. Fear that she'd never see her mother again.

"Lisbeth, darling. What's wrong?"

With a deep sniff, I emerged from the memory still standing in my doorway and Othello's hand was on my shoulder. I shrugged him off, wiping at the tears that had appeared during my throwback. "Sorry," I mumbled to him and sniffed a few times. "See you tomorrow." I closed the door on him and sank slowly to the carpet. My old friend, this ugly expensive carpet. You haven't yet experienced what it's like for me to be on top of you for weeks on end until your fibers are melded into my skin. Let's hope it never comes to that.

"You okay?" Cameron was behind me, wearing a shirt this time, and I stood, straightening up to my full height, trying to smile at him.

"I'm great. I just have some things to do today. You okay

on your own?" Leaving him would be torture, but he was alive now. I wasn't going to let him die again. Never again.

"I'm not a goldfish that dies if you look away," he snarked with that perfect grin of his.

"Right, well, better get downstairs, that orange juice won't drink itself," I said with a gesture to the door.

"Don't you need to feed?" he asked before moving towards the door. "You rescheduled the turning, so you'll need some blood."

"I'll be fine. What's one day without blood?" I shrugged and hooked his arm to usher him out, closing the door behind him. Unbeknownst to him, Arthur and I had gladly gone hungry sometimes to make sure our children had enough blood from their father. Humans had been scarce before and he was the best candidate for blood. Always being thirsty had become somewhat normal to me, but I'd need more if I wanted to use my powers constantly.

After getting dressed into the least fashionable outfit I had, blue jeans with a blue jean jacket, a plain black tee, and boots designed by someone of zero notoriety, I compiled a list of things I needed as I packed a backpack with clothes and other things.

With my bag almost full, I automatically went to my nightstand drawer for the christening artifacts from my children's ceremonies, because that's exactly where I would've kept it here. The drawer only had a brush and some mints, and though my brain threatened to be overcome from everything happening to me, I squared my shoulders and left my room behind.

⚔—

DOWN IN THE KITCHEN, I was packing up some snacks when Olivier entered through the side door that opened up to the patio outside. Looking almost identical to the Olivier from my old life, minus a few scars here and there, she saw me stuffing my backpack as full as it would go with granola bars and twinkies, and leaned against the counters, placing a hand on her hip.

"Going somewhere?"

"Yeah," I said absently, focused on this task so I could be focused on the next until the tasks ended and my family was back in my arms.

"Roses, huh?"

I chanced a look up at her and she had a knowing look on her face. Oh, right. Othello. I tried an ironic laugh that came out like a limp noodle. "Roses, yep," I said, popping my lips with the last syllable while zipping up my bag.

"Lis." I timidly met her eyes to see she had a expression of gentle concern, an emotion that both versions of Olivier rarely displayed. "What's the matter? And what in god's name are you wearing?"

Crossing the distance between us, I swept her up in a hug and wished I could tell her everything. I knew what had happened last time, I'd put her at risk with my secrets, and if

I saved Simon again, she'd be recruited to hunt me down again.

Oh god, Arthur.

I had to get out of here. I needed to go back home so I could tell them all I loved them so much. Selene said it was a one way trip, but there's no way that could be true. She did it once, she can do it again.

"I love you, Olivier. You're my best friend," I whispered against her shoulder. Her timid hands came up to embrace me back and I felt the questions building up inside her over my behavior. I pulled away and left before she could search my eyes again and see everything I was trying to hide. I made the journey down to the basement where the turned dormitory and its rows of empty coffins greeted me. They should be full of newly turned vampires, but that hadn't happened yet. I was changing things already. Was that good or bad? Would it effect the future I came from?

Trotting as fast as I could, I got to the underground garage and clicked the fob to light up the car that belonged to me. It wasn't my old Excalibur. Maybe we'd meet again on this new journey. I pulled up and out of the garage where the front gates opened up for me automatically, then I turned left and sped off down the deserted country road because I had one more stop before finding Highborn.

I had to talk to Balthazar.

3

HIGHBORN

hen I was far enough away from the castle, I stopped my car off the side of the road and got out, traversing down the ditch to a field of prickly grass. Then I breathed deeply and spoke the words Balthazar taught me.

"*Balzjanyóur nappnia lanliápob*[1]," I shouted as loudly as I could. A puff of lilacs smacked me in the face and Balthazar appeared before me with his tailored suit and cane that he tapped against his shiny leather shoe. He was instantly wary of me, his blue eyes running up and down me to find what was different.

"I never taught you how to do that," he said, squinting at me. "You're not my Lisbeth. You're *a* Lisbeth, but not mine. Where did you come from?"

A sigh of relief escaped my lips. I knew it wouldn't be this easy with the other two men, but Balthazar I could always count on. "The future. Specifically, sixty-seven years into the future."

His eyebrows raised in surprised as he tapped more with the cane. "What's it like?"

"It blows. Literally, like…" I motioned with my hands in an explosion gesture, making the sound with my mouth. *Bwooookkksshh.* "Apocalypse happened. Humans are almost extinct. You were put in jail, that was nice, especially since I tasked you with watching someone important to me and you were arrested before I could get back to him." I waited for Balthazar to say something, but he was studying me carefully, picking up on things I'd said, and more importantly things I *hadn't* said.

"There's only one reason I'd be arrested," he noted, his eyes narrowing. "Who was the person you left me with? Boyfriend?" I didn't answer, and that told him enough. "Son then."

"We're not talking about that."

"Then what *are* we talking about?" A small grin pulled at the corners of his mouth and my stomach flipped over. I'd forgotten how much he used to flirt with me before we had sex. Once that happened, everything between us was strictly business. I'd also forgotten how attractive I used to find him.

I cleared my throat and brushed at one of my curls to distract the growing warmth in my mid-section. "I've been sent back by the witches." His eyebrows raised in shock again, but he remained silent. "Apparently the apocalypse wiped them out completely and they were guarding some kind of portal or some crap, and everything was going to shit if it remained unguarded. I don't know, she died before I could get clarification."

He humphed out an ironic laugh. "Should've known the witches would get involved with us sooner or later. Non-involvement treaty, my ass."

"You knew witches existed and you never fucking told me?" I hissed at him, ready to bring a hand out to smack him as punishment for withholding. "You and your fucking secrets, I swear to god. First my grandmother and now this?"

That stopped him cold and he stepped forward to grab my arm with a dark look on his face. "What did future me tell you about her? How much do you know?"

I pried his fingers off me before he left a bruise. "Everything. The Countess, Anastasia. I know everything." He stepped away like I'd slapped him, stumbling back and using his cane to steady himself. "Future us had no secrets. Except for the witches, I suppose. Where did they come from, by the way?"

"Where all the other creatures did. Demons mixing with humans."

"Other creatures?" I spit between clenched teeth. "You'd better start talking, you incorporeal piece of ass."

"You realize that's not an insult."

"TALK."

He rolled his eyes at me. "Fine. When your psycho mother almost destroyed vampires and werewolves, vampires decided to remain closed off from the rest of the world. They didn't want to be involved with witches, centaurs, faeries, the unicorns, or any of them."

"Unicorns are real?"

"Focus," he ordered with a stern look. "So the magical world agreed to cut your kind off from theirs. You were never to know they existed because the magical beasts are at war with witches. They have been for as long as you've been alive. Something happened between them that I was never told about. I'm not even sure they remember anymore. But because vampires were almost destroyed, they wanted to stay out of it. Your kind couldn't afford to lose more people ever. Even though Lycans are part of the magical war, it wasn't possible to erase them from vampire society because of how close your two species are."

Pacing the prickly grass, I clutched a hand to my aching forehead and tried to wrap my mind around this information. "Okay. But, I was part of the vampire Council in my timeline. They never told me any of this."

"Of course they wouldn't have. Most of them don't even know about it. Those that did are sworn to secrecy. The witches put a spell on the vampires so they'd never mention it unless someone else did first. I cautioned they should do the same for Anastasia's story, but they insisted they couldn't just in case she came back. I'm guessing she did." His spiteful tone brought my eyes back to him with a sharp glare.

"Not in the way you think. She saved us. She's actually pretty cool now."

He laughed loudly, ironically, like I was hilarious. "Your future sounds ridiculous. There's no way Anastasia Bathory is *'pretty cool.'*"

I crossed my arms over my chest and gave him a teasing smile. "Haha, laugh it up, Incubus. She's related to you in my future."

He froze and looked up at me, still bent in a laugh. "How?"

Fuck. I bit my lip and tried to keep my face straight. "Never mind. Forget I said that." I couldn't tell him about Kitty. He might never have sex with me and I needed her back.

His warm, appreciative grin sent a jolt right through me. "I never knew you would become an enigma. I have to admit, it is very appealing."

I tried to focus on the ugly grass around us so he wouldn't see a flush on my face. Why was I blushing? *This sucked.* "Yes, well. Feel free to disappear, but remember I can summon you anytime I want, and yes, I'll be doing it often."

His smile grew until it was as bright as the sunlight. "I will be looking forward to it. See you soon, Lisbeth." And he was gone, with only his footprints in the grass to show he'd been there.

God damn it.

Not only had the father of my oldest daughter kept secrets from me all this time, he was also flirting with me again. The last conversation I had with my husbands notwithstanding, I wasn't sure how to handle him staring at me like I was a damn Twinkie.

With the look on his face hammered into my head, I got back into my car and started driving in the direction the magic compass was pointing. I could only hope Highborn was nearby, but it could've very well been in a different country. Selene hadn't told me where it was.

When I checked the compass needle again, it started spinning in every direction. I thumped it against the wheel to fix it and a glowing purple cloud appeared in front of my car, swallowing me up and spitting me out somewhere completely different. I slammed on the brakes as an invisible barrier rose up to meet me, crushing the front of my car. Cursing under my breath, I got out to assess the damage when a ripple went through the barrier and I could see what was behind it for a brief moment.

Hogwarts.

I was at fucking Hogwarts.

That fucking *witch* sent me to a fictional place and now I'd never be able to get back home.

"You there! How did you get here?" A woman stood at a nearby entrance gate that was no doubt the only way to get through the barrier. She had a long, purple dress on and a wand in her hand, so I was definitely in the right place. The school disappeared until all I could see was plain and indifferent countryside. The witch was fast approaching me, holding her wand out like a sword. "We don't allow your kind here, vampire. I'll have to wipe your memory of this place and send you on your way."

"You touch my head and you'll be in all sorts of trouble, lady," I warned, and held up the compass so she could see it. "I'm on a mission. Selene Halace sent me."

Her thin, razor-like eyebrows raised so high they were going to get caught in her hair. "Halace sent you? Halace doesn't know any vampires."

"Look, I'm really tired of this day, so can you just show me inside? Believe me, I would've rather never known your kind exists, because if I didn't, I'd still be back in 2084 with my family, instead of being here where they don't exist."

Impossibly, her eyebrows rose even higher. "2084." I nodded so hard my hair fell over my face and I had to swipe it back. "Come with me." She turned and we walked through the entrance gate, revealing again the massive school building sitting on top of a large hill.

"You realize this place looks like Hogwarts, right?" I noted dryly, looking everywhere at once so I could take it all in.

She humphed at me like a strict schoolmarm. "*It does not.* That place is completely different. Don't let me catch you saying that to our headmaster either, he takes offense." Her long dress hit my legs if I walked too close behind her so I stayed a few paces back. "I'm Isabelle Wisniewski, by the way."

"Lisbeth Bathory."

We'd just reached the front courtyard when she turned

with a look of horror, the name clearly sparking a reaction. "You're not related to that... to Anastasia Bathory, are you?"

Leaning in close to her head, I could smell the succulent blood in her veins, feel the rapid beating of her heart. "She's my mom," I whispered with a grin.

"Oh!" She popped a hand to her mouth. "Oh my." Her eyes darted to the various children in the courtyard around us, no doubt wondering if she had enough time to get them to safety before I attacked them. I would've been amused, if the idea of harming a child wasn't so utterly repulsive to me.

"Relax, Isabelle. I might be a vampire but we have very strict rules about attacking humans. Plus, I'm one of the few who refuses to hurt children. It's gotten me into trouble, too, I can assure you."

Her shoulders relaxed and she managed to smile back at me. "I'm very glad to hear that." We continued on like we'd never stopped and she opened the massive front doors for us, leading up to the entry way where a class of students were standing. "Thank you for waiting, class. Theresa," she addressed to a taller one who approached us. "I need you to stay with the children for now." They discussed a few other things, leading me to believe Theresa was Isabelle's teaching assistant. I zoned out as I waited, looking over the group of kids. They were all about the size Gwen had been, and I stopped cold when I saw a girl that resembled her. Her dark tanned skin, her long black hair, they were the same. But it wasn't her.

What if I never got her back?

"Lisbeth," Isabelle addressed, bring me out of my haze and back to her face. "Come with me, please." I took one last look at the girl and followed her teacher out of the hall.

We went up a flight of stairs, down a hallway, up more stairs, until Isabelle opened a door and led us inside. It looked to be a potions classroom, and three people stood around a cauldron that had bubbling green liquid inside. A large bubble of it burst, sending a drop sailing to the table it sat on, and it sizzled as it ate at the wood. *Gross.* What was in that? Magical acid?

When I looked up from the cauldron, I recognized one of the three standing in front of it. "You," I spat at a younger looking Selene. "You're the one who brought me here."

Of course, this version of her had never seen me before, which she demonstrated by laughing at me with a hand in front of her mouth. "I have no idea what you're—" I interrupted her by holding up the compass and her face turned pale.

One of the other three was a man who was barely taller than my navel. "I'm Headmaster Cauldron. That compass is a magical artifact, it belongs to the school. Where did you get it?"

I pointed a finger to Selene and tossed the compass to Cauldron so he could inspect it. "You took me from my home sixty-seven years in the future. I'd like to know why I'll never see my children again."

The compass started floating above Cauldron's hands and a strange glow came from it. "There's a message inside," he said as he squinted at something I couldn't see. He chanted some odd words and the compass top opened, then suddenly another version of Selene was there with us like a hologram.

"My name is Selene Halace. An apocalyptic level event has all but destroyed life on the planet. My fellow witches and I have protected the portal for as long as we could, but after humans attacked us, I am now the last witch alive, and though I have done everything I can to extend my life, I will not live forever. If the portal remains unguarded, demons will be unleashed on the world, and Earth as we know it will be destroyed." She winced and I could see the bloodied wound she'd had when I met her. "I've been dealt a fatal blow, and I will use the last of my magic to find her: Lisbeth Bathory, the leader of the vampires. If I can discover her hiding place, I will send her back to the past and hope that she can stop Alistair from destroying the planet again." Another audible wince came from her and she doubled over in pain, pressing a hand to her side. "If I can't find her in time, all will be lost. I've recorded this message in the hopes my mission succeeds. Please, help the vampires stop Alistair at any cost, or this future will happen again and everything will be lost." The message cut off and she disappeared, leaving the younger Selene slack jawed with shock.

"I sent you here? I used a time travel spell?" I nodded and her lips pinched together. "I don't have the power level for that. It would've killed me." She trailed off, realizing that's exactly what had happened. Clearing her throat, she continued. "Jasmine is the only one here who could use that spell and not die." Her finger pointed to the other person in the room, a young girl with wild curls similar to mine that had pink tips like Sara's hair.

"It's Jaz, Professor Halace," she remarked, setting off an eye roll from the older woman. "And yeah, I have the power level, but my specialty wouldn't allow it. I'd have to be divination like Halace."

I asked the question that was burning a hole inside me. "So you can't send me back?" All four of the witches looked uncomfortable and met my eyes with regret, killing all the hope I'd had up to that point.

It was Cauldron who said something to break the tension. "Time travel spells can only go to the past."

Halace looked the most regretful. "Surely I explained that to you," she said quietly. My eyes filled with tears I didn't want to hold back, with several falling off my lashes when I shook my head.

"I just want my babies back," I sobbed weakly, an overwhelming need to curl up into a ball rising inside me. If I stayed that way forever, maybe I could forget this nightmare. "You said I could get them back."

Without another word, she spun on her heels and walked quickly to one of the shelves in the room, putting aside specimen jars and opening books, looking for something. "Jaz, get a fresh cauldron ready."

Unable to keep standing with this news, I found a nearby chair and sank into it. The headmaster walked up to me and took my hand, patting it with his own tiny one.

"I'm sure what we've done must seem insignificant to losing your family. Please know that protecting the portal to the demon world is vital to the survival of this planet. We would not have destroyed your future if there had been any other way."

I wanted to take my hand back, but he was trying to be kind, and that kept me from bolting away from his touch. "I've already lost everything trying to save this world. Now I've lost everything again. But…" I trailed off, shutting my eyes and swallowing hard. "Before I had my children, I only cared about protecting the humans. And now I've lost them to protect humans once again."

"How many children, vampire?" Selene tossed at me from her work.

I felt too defeated to ponder her motive behind the question. "Four."

She nodded, still working on picking up things from the shelves. "Headmaster, I need you to perform a grab and go spell," she barked as Jaz hauled a cauldron onto the table beside the acid one.

He seemed to know what she was getting at because he let go of my hand. "How long have you been back in this time?"

My head was aching but I remembered what time I'd gotten up. "About an hour. Maybe two."

"Perfect," he said, rolling up his brown sleeves. "The longer you're here, the more your future gets degraded. It's already almost gone, but we can bring one, maybe two items back here." I pushed forward in excitement, but he held out a hand to stop me short. "Not a person. Now, think of something that has DNA from all of your children. We'll need it for what Halace is making."

It wasn't hard to think of what we needed: a necklace I'd worn every day for years, but that last day I'd left it on the dresser because I was in a hurry. "A necklace," I answered. "It has some of their hair in it."

Cauldron slapped his hands together, spoke a few words, and a glowing ball formed between them that he expanded by pulling his hands apart. "Come over here, take my arm. Tell me where you left it." I put a hand on his small arm and pictured the dresser in my head, the cherry wood, and the necklace on top of it. "That's it," he said in triumph, reaching his hand inside the glowing ball and pulling it back out with my necklace clasped in his tiny fingers. "Heads up," he shouted, throwing the necklace behind him where Selene caught it without looking, still bent over the cauldron. "We have enough time for a second item. Preferably something to stop Alistair."

"I don't..." I squished my eyes shut to think of something, anything. A memory of my mother's house came with her personal journal on a shelf, one she'd used during her quest to find him all those years ago. "It's a journal in my mother's house."

"It's not yours?" he said with gritted teeth, seemingly struggling to keep the glowing ball between his hands.

"It's harder to bring back items that don't belong to you,"

Isabelle explained, kneeling next to us and putting a hand on the headmaster's other arm. "Here, you can use some of my magic to find it."

I pictured the journal in her house and the headmaster started sprouting drops of sweat on his forehead. "This part of the future is too degraded. Think of a different time when you saw the journal, something closer to this one." I remembered when everyone had returned from finding Balthazar, Anastasia had kept the journal in her backpack, and I saw it when she put her bag down to grab a slice of cake. "Got it!" Cauldron shouted, reaching into the glow again and coming out with the book in his hand. The glow disappeared and he staggered back, catching his breath and wiping the sweat from his forehead. "Ahh, shit. That spell is so hard."

"Language," Isabelle chastised with her lips pressed together.

He waved a hand at her in dismissal, handed me the journal, and sat down hard on the cold stone floor next to us. "We can't do it again, you understand," he told me as he leaned back against his hands.

"I do." I looked up over his head and saw Selene opening my necklace to take some of the hairs out while Jaz stirred the pot. "Can I have that back when you're done?" She nodded, ignoring me, too engrossed in what she was brewing. "What is she making?"

Selene checked a book and added a few leaves of something into the cauldron. "It's a life potion, made specifically to bring back children someone has lost. Time travel isn't done very often, but we do have ways to help the traveler. This is what I was talking about when I told you we could get your children back." I hopped up, eager to see the process that would bring my family back.

Jaz smiled at me, still stirring the potion, and I could see a trail of magic coming from her hand and down the spoon to the mixture. "I'm a necromancer, so life and death are my thing."

"Yes, well, I'd do this one myself but I'm not powerful enough, plus it needs a necromancer's life power," Selene grumbled, adding something that looked like a dried toad. "You're lucky we have one. There hasn't been a necromancer for four hundred years until Jaz came here." She checked her book and turned to me with another question. "How many of the children are with the same father?" Surprisingly, she didn't seem judgmental with that question.

"Two."

"We'll need two bottles then, if you would, Isabelle." Isabelle got up and floated over to one of the shelves where she found a big bottle and a smaller one that she put next to the cauldron. Jaz kept stirring until the potion turned bright pink and Selene checked one more time in the book before dropping the hairs inside, making it turn as purple as my eyes. She leaned back, satisfied, and got out a ladle to start pouring into the bottles.

"I umm..." I started, and they all looked up at me from their work. "I had a bit of difficulty conceiving with one of my husbands, it took nineteen years for me to have our son.

Will this fix that?" I didn't want to wait that long to have all of my babies back.

Thankfully, Selene slowly smiled and continued fixing the bottles up. "I added a little something that will aid in conception, you shouldn't have any trouble this time around. In fact, you might find yourself pregnant quite quickly between births if you're not careful."

"And why two bottles?" I asked as she handed the larger bottle to Isabelle.

"One dose will get the three with different fathers, but in order to conceive with one of them a second time, the potion needs to be reapplied. So, you'll drink the large one first, and when you want to have the fourth child, you'll drink the smaller one."

Isabelle corked the larger bottle. "Selene, you're explaining it wrong. She's going to think all she has to do is drink it."

"I'm sure I understand having a child takes more than drinking something," I said, unable to not be a smart mouth. Jaz laughed and the teachers glared at her for it.

"My apologies," Selene said, adding one other thing to the cauldron before filling the smaller one up as well. "There is something else needed for this potion to work, thank you, Isabelle." She took the bottles and handed them to me. They felt warm, like a heartbeat. "You have to get all three of the fathers to fall in love with you for it to work. Real, romantic love. Not friend love, not family love."

"Can't be boner love either," Jaz said, making them glare

at her again. "Hey, I'm an adult. Leave me alone."

Selene held up a warning finger to her pupil before looking back at me. "If it's only two of the three that love you, it won't do anything. And you have to love them romantically as well, that's also important. You'll know it's worked when you feel an icy burning warmth in your belly for each pregnancy."

"There's one other thing, and I'm hoping future Selene told you this," Cauldron said as he came to stand beside me, looking up at me as I looked down at him. "You'll get the same children back, but they won't be the same children you knew. They could be a different orientation, different mentality, different personality, different powers. The only thing we can guarantee is that you will give birth to the child you had before."

I studied the bottles in my hands and clutched my fingers around them. "That's enough for me. Details are nothing. As long as I get them back."

"You should take the larger one now," Selene said, starting to pick up her supplies. "I put something extra in the smaller one so it stays potent for about five to ten years. Don't delay on that one or we'll have to make another. If it stops being purple it's not viable anymore."

I uncorked the larger bottle and held it to my lips. It smelled like old shoes, but I downed it without throwing up. "Oh god, that's gross."

"To having kids," Jaz said, holding out a fist bump for me that I gratefully accepted.

4

SAVING SIMON

*F*our cups of tea in Headmaster Cauldron's office hadn't dulled the taste the potion left on my tongue. After they fixed my car and found the location of a few people for me, they opened up a portal back to the road outside the castle and gave me a locket that would open another portal if I needed to find them for anything.

Back near the castle, I sat on the side of the road staring at the purple filled bottle in my hand. With my children fixed, I had several missions now. I had to find Knight and make him love me. I had to bring Arthur here and make him love me. I had to convince Balthazar to love me in a non-family way, not to mention I had to fall in love with him in that way too. And I had to rally the vampires to find and defeat Alistair.

I could do this. The end goal was seeing my kids again. I could do this for them.

The second end goal was being with my husbands again. The last thing I'd said to them was *'stick it up your ass.'* If they didn't end up with me this time around, no matter if it meant not having my children again, I'd forever remember my pathetic send-off to them.

Unwilling to go home since everything was so off about being back there, I decided on spending the night in my car. It proved difficult because I hadn't fallen asleep without either of my husbands beside me in decades, and I longed for their scents to wrap around me and lull me to a gentle sleep in their embrace. After tossing and turning almost all night, I woke up late the next morning from the phone alarm I'd set so I could make sure I was in town at least ten minutes before Simon.

"Hello, Lisbeth." Balthazar was suddenly sitting in the passenger seat of my car, smelling like a truckload of lilacs. "You smell different. Did you do something?" He leaned into me, sniffing hard at my unwashed body, and my stomach fluttered the way it used to when Knight was with me. Even after all our time together, every time my Alpha was near me I'd had the same reaction.

I moved away from Balthazar's nose, hating that I was reacting like that when Knight and Arthur still hadn't met me. "No, I didn't do anything. Move away, I can't drive with you like that." I turned the car on and started driving towards town. I had a child to save.

He shook a triumphant finger and smiled to himself. "You smell fertile. That's what it is."

"Ewww, what the fuck? You can't smell that."

"Who says?"

Damn it. "Why are you here? You weren't here the first time I did this." We pulled into the town and I navigated through the streets to find the right block.

"The first time you did what?" he asked, looking around us for something exciting we were about to do.

"Broke the law," I answered, coming to a stop in a parking spot about a block away from where I knew Simon would be. I chanced a quick look at Balthazar and he was looking at me appreciatively, warmly, like he never knew how awesome I was, which was ridiculous because I'd always been awesome. "Stop staring at me like that." I turned back to the intersection in front of us and thrummed my hands on the steering wheel.

"You're low on blood," he observed beside me.

"I'm used to it. It's not a big deal. I'll drink later." Every movement of someone coming around the corner of the intersection made me jump, but they still weren't here yet. I checked my watch and opened my door, getting out when it was safe to cross the street. Balthazar followed close behind me and we walked down the sidewalk, getting closer to the spot that had changed my life forever. We stopped there and I leaned against the bus stop bench that was nearby, waiting on pins and needles.

What if they didn't come? How else would I get Arthur

here? There was no way to find him unless Othello gave me his phone number, and I doubted Arthur would care enough to come to the stuffy castle for some airhead girl.

Maybe if I had a phrase I could say to him that would convince him I'm telling the truth about knowing him. Now that I thought about it, I knew exactly what I would say, but Simon and the Lycans were in front of me before I had to contemplate going back home and talking to Othello.

As before, Simon crossed the street ahead of his parents, and his Alpha shouted for him to come back, but he was a child who wanted to do his own thing no matter what. We were waiting for him when he stepped onto the sidewalk and bumped into me for a second time.

"Simon!" his dad shouted across the crosswalk, unable to come forward without forfeiting his life to me. He glared at me, baring his teeth in a feral growl, and Alexander stopped him with a hand on his chest. I didn't look surprised this time, and they weren't terrified of me as they'd been before. They were angry, but they weren't stupid. They stayed put as they waited for me to decide what to do.

"Simon," I told the boy with his short, mussy black hair, and he stared up at me, looking almost exactly like my Jason. "The law says I have to kill Lycans that cross into vampire territory, as you have just done." I knelt down to be level with his little head. "You look like my son." My hands itched to reach out and push his hair back, but I kept them firmly on my lap, clasped so tightly my nails dug into my skin. "I've been on this earth for a very long time, and there is only one rule I have for myself, one I would do anything to uphold. I don't kill children. Not even you." My chin trembled and I struggled to hold myself together.

"Because of your son?" Simon asked me. I realized that was the first time I'd heard his voice before he grew to an adult, and he sounded so much like Jason, I wanted to die.

"No," I told him. "Because you're worth protecting, no matter what you are." With shaking limbs, I stood and held out a hand for the boy to take, and I walked him up to the middle of the street where the vampire border ended. Simon eagerly went to his mother's arms while I met Alexander's thoughtful gaze.

"Why are you letting the boy go?"

Seeing the Lycan again after so long brought a smile to my face and I wanted so much to hug him. "You heard what I said." The repeat of my words had come without me thinking.

"Your kind will find out," Alexander cautioned as he had before.

"I'm counting on it. You should go now." I gestured off in the other direction and waited for them to go, but as he had done the first time, Alexander started undoing his vampire teeth bracelet. I stopped him before he could get it unclasped. "No, you can keep that."

His hands dropped and he studied me again, closely, trying to figure me out. "This will protect you against my kind. We owe you a debt."

"I didn't save Simon for a reward. I saved him because it

was the right thing to do." My fingers tapped against my legs, I was starting to become anxious we would be discovered by whoever snitched on me before. "Maybe…" I looked around, just in case there was a vampire nearby. "Maybe one day we'll be allies. Maybe one day our species will stop fighting and make peace. I want that more than I want your gratitude."

"I'll take your name, then. That's all I want."

"Alexander, we have to leave," Simon's father growled out, edging them away while reaching a hand out to his Alpha.

"Lisbeth," I told my old friend. "Now go." They left, rounding a corner and disappearing into safety. I stayed long enough to make sure no one ran after them, and I turned to see Balthazar standing so close to me, he could've licked my nose with his tongue.

"What was that?"

I stepped back and straightened my jacket, hoping my cheeks weren't as flushed as my insides were. "I saved him before. It'll bring someone I need to the castle. I had to save him again or that person won't come."

"Not that. The son. You weren't just saying that, you had a child in the future. I could see it when you looked at the boy, you were seeing your child's face. I know what that looks like, I felt it with your grandmother, and now every time I see your face, I see her."

If he kept holding a candle for her, he'd never love me back. I'd never see my children again.

"I'm not my fucking grandmother," I snapped at him,

unable to hold it in. "I'm a real person, and if you respected her at all, you would love me for me and not because of her."

Taken aback, he blinked and looked away. "I've always loved you for you. Can't believe future me never told you that." He turned back to me and I focused on his cravat so I wouldn't have to see his eyes. "When is this person coming?"

"Tomorrow night." Only one day and I'd see my Arthur again, with his scarred face and his impossibly stubborn-ass attitude. I needed his strength to get through this, especially if finding Knight didn't go well. "I can't fucking wait that long, I'm on pins and needles as it is." My phone went off with a text from Marie telling me to get my ass to the castle because they couldn't delay the turning any longer.

Fuck me twice. God, I really had to play house until Arthur arrived, didn't I?

Growling, I put my phone back into my jeans pocket and held up the Vulcan salute for the Incubus. "Live long and prosper, Balthy. I'll be at the castle if you need me."

"Balthy?" he scoffed, and disappeared in a huff, leaving me with only the scent of lilacs blowing against my face.

It took little more than ten minutes to get back home and I made sure to use the front garage entrance so I would enter straight into the turned dormitory where everyone was already gathered around the humans chosen to become vampires. Almost all of the Born vampires gave me dirty looks for being late and I kept my eyes down until I had navigated through the group to Olivier. She had her dreads in a thick braid and her mermaid dress on, looking exactly like she used to, and was giving me a pointed stare as she tapped her long nails on one of her dark arms.

"Where have you *been*? Othello has almost put out a search party for you. He's not happy."

Unbeknownst to her, he'd also probably already been informed about the incident at the border, considering how quickly Arthur arrived after what I'd done the first time. Othello was glaring disapprovingly at me over the crowd, but I smiled back until he softened just a bit. I wasn't on trial yet, I still had some leeway with him.

Without a speech, since he thought speeches were self-serving, Othello motioned we begin with a flick of his hand.

My stomach growled even though my thirst was completely under control. I could've gone much longer before I needed blood, but I wasn't about to say no to a three day supply. I'd be able to use my powers for a week with that.

Eagerly, I sank my fangs into the first human, drinking deeply and taking my usual daily amount from all three of my assigned humans. No one would notice my power level rising since I knew how to mask it, and I needed the extra blood for everything ahead of me.

Once the humans were fed from, I let them drink a small mouthful of my blood, and then it began. Again.

The humans all hit the deck and writhed in pain as the vampire blood worked through their systems. I impatiently waited for them to stop moving, tapping my fingers against the three blood packs Olivier had given me until the humans were temporarily dead, and gasping along with them when they came back to life.

This was the most tedious day ever.

After the new vampires stood up, we gave them the blood packs to drink. Once they'd had their first taste of blood, I assisted the bigger Born vampires with wrangling up the newly turned and stuffing them into their coffins. It was something I never helped with before because I'd been too delicate and wore fancy clothes.

I wasn't delicate anymore.

Olivier gave me more than a few looks as we wrestled one vampire into his coffin before we shut and locked the lid. "When did you get so tough?" she asked me, like it was a normal day and a vampire hadn't just sliced her cheek open. I motioned to the spot and she held the skin together until it reformed again, leaving a thin, pink line on her perfect skin.

"I'm a pirate, remember?" I grinned, calling back to when we'd first met and the pirate Olivier had taken me under her wing so we could bash around Europe together for decades. She met my grin and held out a fist for a fist bump, something she rarely did. "Where's Renard? Are he and Cameron lifting weights again?" We watched a group of Born vampires struggling to put the last turned in his coffin, so we rushed over to help and locked it for them once he was inside. His fists beat against the thick wood and he screamed that we were vampire whores and he was going to murder us once he get out. Not that I was excusing his words, but I'd heard much worse during this stage of the turning. I casually leaned against the coffin and smiled at my best friend. "Wanna get a drink?"

"You're acting weird," she observed, but she was still relaxed in her stance so she didn't suspect me yet.

My instant reaction was a Knight worthy retort of repeating her words back. He had really rubbed off on me. Not that I was complaining. "I heard someone broke the law," I said casually, trailing my hand over the coffin and ignoring the screaming coming from inside it. "I was wondering if you'd heard the same?"

That was when her eyebrow slowly lifted and her stance changed. Shit, she was onto me. "No, I haven't heard anything like that. Who told you?"

I made a raspberry noise with my lips and shrugged my shoulders up and down. "I was walking in the hallway and I heard someone talking about it. When I went to check, they were gone. Can't say who it was."

Her eyes narrowed and I almost ran away so she'd stop looking at me like that. "Why do you care?"

I put an offended hand to my chest. "I'm the second in command here. Plus, they said something about a vampire Hunter coming. Some hard ass dude." I almost mentioned he was her ex, but she would've known I knew something because that wasn't common knowledge.

She leaned against the coffin beside mine and I breathed a sigh of relief when she slightly relaxed her stance. "His name is Arthur. He's only sent in when someone from an Order breaks the law."

"As I said, I heard that happened." I let a few seconds pass, tapping my finger still. "So do you think they'll send him here?"

"Again, why do you care so much?"

Because I needed the fucker to fall in love with me and impregnate me. You know, normal stuff.

"I'm taking an interest in this Order now and I'm wary of someone coming here that I don't know, call it paranoia. Will you tell me if he's coming?" I bit my lip and tried not to show how anxious I was about her saying no.

Instead, she shrugged and I slipped off her radar. "Sure, whatever. You mentioned drinks, let's go do that." She turned and I followed her out, pumping my fist in a tiny victory.

5

ENTER ARTHUR

A drink with Olivier quickly turned into us getting as
smashed as possible in my suite, because anything
less would mean I was awake enough to think, and I was
tired of thinking. I just needed Arthur with me, then everything else would turn out okay.

I woke up with a hangover, feeling worse than I had the
night before. As the turned were still cooking in their tombs
all day, Olivier went to do some paperwork while I sat in the
foyer of the castle, watching the sun rise and waiting for
Arthur to arrive.

What if he didn't come? Everything would be ruined.

It was lunchtime before Cameron came by and sat next to
me. "Hey, you. What's up? You and Olivier got drunk all over
the living room. The carpet smells like vodka now. Kind of
an improvement though."

I wrapped my hands around my bent knees and rested my chin on them, feeling utterly defeated. "Everything sucks and I'm dying inside."

He bumped my shoulder with his. "Oh, well, if it's only that, then you're fine."

I smiled despite my mood and leaned my head onto his shoulder. I'd missed him so much, and he was here with me again. That thought had me turning and putting my arms around his warm body, resting on the crook of his neck. "What if I can't fix it all?" I sniffed and snuggled closer, drinking in the scent of him, the one I'd lost.

He chuckled, his chest bumping up and down against my ear, not even phased by my words, as if the world sucking was a normal occurrence for us. "You're Lisbeth. You raised me right, right? You can do anything."

"That's what they used to say," I whispered, holding in any tears trying to escape.

"Who's they?" he asked, but the front door opened, interrupting us. I jumped up, only to see it was just a companion holding some grocery bags.

Fucking hell. When was he coming? I couldn't take this.

"I'm going to the gym," I announced, walking up the staircase next to us.

Cameron stood, looking at me like I just said I was going to eat bugs. "You never go there."

"Shut up and come with me."

We changed in our room, and I had to make do with a sports bra and some yoga pants since I didn't have workout gear. Cameron followed me back down to one of the areas in the castle I'd rarely gone to before.

The gym had several vampires inside, as well as a few humans, all lifting weights or working out. I was more interested in the fighting mat. Being Arthur's mates meant Knight and I had been his sparring partners, and we'd both learned to defend ourselves a long time ago, before Salvation was even a thought in our heads. We picked up the training after Gwen was born, and I had to admit, I was very good at it.

I wasn't the soft-bellied girl I was before. I was a warrior.

I surveyed the room, noting the exits and any weapons I could use just in case, something Arthur had hammered into my head many times. I braided my long curls into a tight French braid and approached the sparring mat. A few big vampires were wrestling on it, just having fun, not really serious about hurting each other, or winning.

I watched them, hands against my bare belly, noting their sloppy techniques with a quirked eyebrow. Arthur would be disgusted. After they'd gotten up and were giving each other high fives, I stepped closer.

"Can I join?" I asked with a friendly smile, and was met with laughter that made me scowl at them. I walked onto the mat, getting in between the two tall men, something I was quite used to. They were both big, but I'd had bigger. *Wink.* "What, you think I can't take you? I'll take you all the way to Sunday school, buddy."

"The fuck does that mean?" one of them asked me, chuckling under his breath again.

As an answer, I launched into him like a missile, punching his solar plexus, elbowing him right on the base of his neck, and bringing my knee up to crunch his nose with an audible snap, then I let him go so he could fall onto the mat in pain. I looked up and saw the other guy starting to sweat, but he was still desperate to prove himself to the other vampires that had gathered around us, so he ran at me and I side stepped at the last second, jumping up on his back and trapping his throat in my elbow where I tugged hard, crushing his windpipe. He beat his hands on me and tried to reach a hand back to grab my hair, but I was ready, pulling his thumb back until it popped out of its socket and he howled in pain. My elbow cutting off his air supply made him pass out, joining his friend on the mat.

Wow, they seriously sucked. They were making me look much better than I actually was, and I was still pretty awesome.

"Who's next?" I challenged, and several of the spectators came at me, putting up a fight until I knocked them all down and rose triumphant, breaking out into a light sweat and pushing some escaped hairs out of my face.

"*Jesus Christ*," someone exclaimed behind me, and I turned, my chest still heaving, to see Olivier standing with a slack faced Arthur.

Arthur.

Without thinking, I ran to him and jumped into his arms only for him to shove me away in surprise because he had no idea who I was. I swallowed the shooting pains in my heart from the vacant look on his face.

"Sorry," I said, still out of breath. "That was a hug check. Just wanted to see how you'd react." I tried to make myself remember he was here to arrest me, but I was just so happy to see him, I couldn't focus on anything else.

"When did you learn to fight like that?" Olivier asked, looking at me like I was an alien.

I waved a modest hand at her. "Oh, you know. Here and there. I mean, we teach the turned how to fight, I figured I might as well learn the basics."

Arthur snorted slightly, belly laughter for him. "You said she was shit at lying. I thought you were joking." He barely looked down at me, still trying to pretend I wasn't there because I hadn't made him notice me yet. "You've been fighting for years. I can tell."

There was one thing he didn't realize, I was very used to his jibes, and I responded the way I always did. "Okay then, you're sparring me. Right now." That got his full attention and he appraised me with his icy blue eyes for the first time. *God damn it*, a powerful shiver was going up my spine and it was all I could do to not launch myself at him and beg him to kiss me.

His face went blank again and I could see him struggle not to laugh at me. "I don't think so. I'm not about to help you break a nail."

"You *just* saw me kick all of their asses and you still think I'm a stuffy rich girl?" He shrugged slightly, staring straight ahead and not looking at me. I planted myself in front of him and stood on my tip toes so he would be forced to meet my eyes. *"Bring it."*

And fuck, the heat between us was about to melt me into a puddle. It was still here, no matter that we hadn't met before in this time, and the fact that I was so aware of him meant I wasn't going to let him push me away this time. He still seemed reluctant, though his chest had started rising with rapid breaths and his heart sped up, so I helped him along with one of the only jibs that worked on him.

"Unless you're a *pussy.*"

His nostrils flared, making me flutter all over. God, just take me right now. I don't care who's watching. With robotic movements, he took his jacket off and dumped his bag on the gym floor. He stalked me like I was his prey as I walked backwards, and he matched me step for step in an erotic dance.

Once my shoes reached the mat, Arthur launched at me, but he wasn't at all like the other men. He'd been watching me, anticipating my movements, and he was ready when I fainted to the side. He grabbed my bare stomach and wrapped himself around me from behind, pinning my legs and arms with his. I whipped my head back and knocked into his face, then I grew my nails so I could sink them into his calves and I tore upwards until he let me go.

Rolling away, I bowled up and stood, holding my claws out in front of me as he got up, looking down at his bloodied jeans and back at me. Was he impressed? That wasn't even my best move. He came at me again, and while he was admittedly better at this than me, as he always had been, I held my own until we'd been sparring for a good half hour and he still hadn't made me surrender.

I never surrendered. I was Lisbeth Fucking Bathory.

Sweaty, tired, and never quite able to catch my breath before he came at me again, I deflected another attack and came at him this time, holding his hands off with mine so we were almost pressed together. This was some wicked foreplay, I had to say.

"If you give in, I'll tell everyone it's because you couldn't hurt a woman," I grunted, his powerful muscles gaining ground against mine.

His icy facade was gone, leaving him open to grin at me. "Not a chance."

"Your loss," I warned, and just to show him how serious I was, I did my best move. With our hands occupied, I twisted in a Beckham move and slammed my leg into his head as hard as I could, then I flipped and wrapped my arms around his legs, pulling them out from under him. He slammed into the mat and I ax stomped my leg into his groin, the one place on his body I hated hurting, but this was war, damn it. If Arthur didn't respect me, he'd never be mine again. Kicking his ass wasn't exactly the best method for other guys, but for Arthur it would work like a charm.

His hands flew to his crotch and he rolled to his side, groaning loudly while the spectators winced in horror, except for Olivier who was cheering me on by Cameron's side. When Arthur resurfaced, I held out a hand to help him up and he did so, keeping his eyes on me like I was a cat prowling to attack again.

"Let's go," he ordered.

Oh fuck yeah! Had I already won him over? Would we have sex somewhere in the castle? I was totally up for that, considering sparring with my husband had me as wet as a faucet.

I fist bumped an impressed Cameron as we passed him and Arthur picked up his stuff on the way out of the gym. I followed him to a side room that was used for hippie meditation and he slammed the door behind us.

"Where in the *fuck* did you learn how to fight like that? That was Hunter level techniques. I've been using some of those moves for decades and I've never taught them to anyone. Who taught you, tell me, *now*!" he shouted at me, making me wince slightly.

"You did."

He scoffed. "I've never met you before. Now stop lying and tell me."

"Chloe."

Arthur froze like I'd hit him with an icy blast, slowly dropping his clenched hands. "What did you just say?"

"I said Chloe. That was her name. The baby you never had with Adriann because you killed her for attacking humans."

He clenched his jaw, trying desperately to control himself

around me, a stranger. "I've never spoken that name out loud before. Never."

My hand reached automatically to clutch the necklace with my children's hair inside, but I wasn't wearing it. I'd left it in my rooms so it wouldn't get broken at the gym. "I've known you for almost seventy years, but you don't remember them at all. The witches sent me back here from the future to prevent the world from ending."

"You're not supposed to know about the witches," he said immediately, an automatic reaction to me mentioning them.

"Great, you know about them too? *God*, Arthur. You never fucking told me about them. You're such an asshole." Now that he knew some of my story, I had no problem talking to him the way I used to.

"I can't mention them audibly unless they're mentioned by someone else first, so I'm not surprised. Besides, why would I trust you enough with that information?"

Glaring at him, I put a hand to my sweaty hip. "You told me about Chloe, I'm very certain that information matters more to you than witches." That shut him up with his lips pressed together. "You have to help me fix the problem from my future, and I can't tell more than a few people because of the non-involvement treaty. I haven't even told Olivier."

"I'm not interested in helping you with anything, and there's only one reason I would've told you about Chloe, and that's if we were mated, but I highly doubt *that* happened."

"Guess what. We were." I blew him a sarcastic kiss.

"You're lying."

"You literally just said I was shit at lying, so I'm sure you can tell that I'm not," I smarted, rolling my eyes at his stubbornness. "God, you're dumb sometimes."

"I'm not sure what I did in the future that made you think you can talk to me like this," he warned, but all it did was make me want to shove him against the wall and make out with him to shut him up.

"I just said we were mated. I know you well enough to know exactly how to talk to you."

His icy eyes looked me up and down, making my cheeks heat when he lingered over certain parts of me. "We've had sex in your future?"

"No, I'm a nun. Of course we've fucked." He stopped at my eyes and I knew he was enjoying the flush on my face. "You're also lovers with my other mate." I left out that he was a werewolf, because that was going to be bad enough on its own.

"Where is he?"

I looked down at Arthur's boots, my lips pinching together to hold the sadness at bay. "We haven't met yet in this time. I'm going to find him as soon as I'm done with you. Hopefully you'll come with me."

"I have to stay here, someone has broken the law."

"Yeah," I said, clicking my tongue and looking back up at him with no shame. "That was me. My bad. But I had to do it again so you'd come here."

"Again? You broke the law where you came from?"

"It's how we met the first time."

58

The rule enforcing Arthur narrowed his eyes at me. "You don't even care, do you?"

I answered with an apathetic shrug. "I saved a child's life. He's not a Lycan yet. So no, I don't care. If I don't live by my own code, then who am I? You can respect that, right?" I knew he could, but he was too focused on the law breaking part. He hadn't become the Arthur that would do anything for me yet, and most of that was because I wasn't part of the Council. "You know what, how about we just convene the Council right now and they'll put me on trial. I know for a fact they'll let me off."

"We can't just *convene* the Council. None of them live here. Now who's the dumb one?"

"Hey," I snapped, shaking a finger at him. "I'm very smart, thank you. Also, it's called Skype. Let's go."

"I don't take orders from you," he informed me, crossing his arms over his chest.

"Oh my *god*, you're even worse than I remembered. Fine, whatever. Follow, or don't, I don't care. I'm going to Othello's office."

I left the room and walked out to the foyer, turned and went straight down the hallway, past Marie's desk where she yelled at me to stop before I opened the double doors and strolled right in.

Othello sat at his desk with a pile of papers and he smiled at me. "Ahh, Lisbeth. I put some daisies in your room this morning."

"Yes, yes, that's great," I told him, hearing Arthur

entering behind me and shutting the doors in Marie's complaining face. I almost felt bad for her since she'd been my mother's mate in the future, but she was still a bitch at the moment. "So, you brought Arthur here because someone broke the law, right?" Othello fumbled, unable to form a response. "It was me. I broke the law. And I request an immediate trial before the Council. Now, as Arthur has mentioned, they're not here, and it'll take a few days to get them in a plane and get rooms ready, blah blah blah, so let's just skip that, shall we?" I turned and walked past Arthur who shot a hand out and grabbed my wrist to make sure I wasn't going to run away. The contact of his fingers made me ache all over for him, but I pushed past it to open the doors again. "Marie, can you come here?" She walked over from her desk, trying to hide a scowl at the sight of me.

"What do you want?" she snarked with just enough of a smile that normal people would've been convinced she was a nice person.

Ahh, mom. You really knew how to pick them.

"I need you to set up a Skype call with the other Orders and get their Heads on the screen. Okie dokie?" She looked behind me at Othello who waved his hand to her so she'd do it. With her scurrying off to her desk, I looked down at Arthur's hand holding me, and back up at him. "You can let me go. I'm not running again." He watched me carefully before dropping his hand, setting my wrist free. I had a sudden deep seated urge to plant myself against him and run my finger up and down the long scar on his cheek, and if Othello hadn't been there, I would've chanced it.

Marie came back in with a laptop and started setting it up on Othello's desk. He looked back at us. "You should wait outside while we get it ready. It might take a few minutes."

Arthur led the way to the waiting room and I paced the floor while he stood still in the doorway, guarding it. "You were in charge here, weren't you. That's why you talked to me like that, why you're ordering Othello and the Council around."

"Guilty," I confessed, still pacing the ugly green carpet. "Othello was kidnapped after my trial last time and I took his place. You were my bodyguard. We fell in love. You ate me out in his office." I met his icy eyes and quickly looked away before he could see me blushing again. "TMI, sorry. But yes, I was in charge. Kind of weird being an underling again when I've carried the fate of vampires on my shoulders for so long." I rested my hands on the back of my neck and tugged on the skin in agitation that they were taking forever. "I once asked you why you followed me. Whether it was because you loved me or because you believed I deserved to be followed. Do you know what you said?"

"Probably something about the one where I'm not emotional all the time?" he guessed, making me double over with mirth.

"God, that is exactly what you said," I laughed, wiping my eyes until I tried to be serious, finding a spot on the maroon walls to stare at. "I asked you because I needed to know if I was a good leader, and if you'd followed me out of love, I knew it meant I wasn't the right person to lead our people. Your opinion is one of the only that I trust."

"Me and your other husband," he mused with a quirk to his lip. I nodded, turning again on the carpet. "There's no guarantee we'll be mated this time around, just to be clear." My feet almost faltered in their path but I tried to keep moving, because if he was right, I'd never get any of my babies back.

"I know." We shared a look and I could tell he was trying to figure me out. I would've settled for making out instead, but hey, I had time.

Marie poked her head out of Othello's office doors. "We're ready for your trial."

Arthur waited for me to pass before turning and coming in beside me, another movement he was repeating from my last trial. We entered the office and saw that Marie had set up a giant television screen with the Skype call, and it had a webcam clipped onto the top. Othello was standing in front of the screen with his hands clasped in front of himself.

"My fellow Council members, I do apologize for this unorthodox trial," he said to them. I noticed Castilla in one screen, along with Thaddeus and Estinien. All twelve, including Othello, were in attendance. They were once my peers. You know, before the world ended and killed most of them. "The accused has requested to speak on her behalf." He moved aside, letting me take his place a few feet from the television.

Castilla looked like she had just rolled out of bed with her coif mussed. "I am Castilla of the Order Acilino."

Oh. My. God. She was not going to repeat everything...

"Elisabeth, you stand accused of disregarding..."

Fuuuuuuck, she was.

I waited patiently until she finished the speech I'd already heard twice, and then mentioned the Othello not being allowed to oversee my trial part that I'd also heard before. I said 'yes' when prompted, and once she was done, I stopped her before she could continue.

"If I may," I offered, and she went silent so I could speak, but I got more than a few glowers from the other Council members for being impertinent. "Look, we all know that if I allow this trial to drag on, you'll spend half a year debating about semantics." Arthur made a noise and I wondered if he'd flick my ear like last time, but he remained still behind me, denying me his touch, even if it was just an ear flick. "The long and short of the matter is that I spared the life of a child. I don't much care that he was a Lycan pup because I don't kill children, Lycan or otherwise. The fact of the matter, however, has nothing to do with my personal convictions that I know will have no bearing on your decision, but instead lie with a detail about this boy. He was human, he smelled human. One day he will become a Lycan, but he is not one yet. I think we can all agree that his current state matters more than his future state, since we pride ourselves on protecting human life above our own, or does that only matter when that human will remain a human until they die?"

Shit. I'd been going for powerful and moving, but I ended up with surly. Maybe they would throw me in jail again or execute me. Well, if Arthur was my jailer, I could think of worse punishments.

They'd all gone silent so I leaned forward and added, "With respect," just in case they thought I was rude enough to execute me for it. With Estinien in the mix, anything was possible.

Castilla was the first to snap out of it, but the respectful look on her face was promising. It was how she used to look at me when I was on the Council making all the decisions. "Arthur, would you please escort Lisbeth out while we discuss her testimony?"

We both left the office and stood in the waiting room where I paced the floor again while Arthur stood guard at the door like I was going to rush in at any moment and kill someone.

"That thing you said about making you wait for six months, that was what happened last time, isn't it," he stated, watching me with his blue eyes.

"Yep. Nearly went insane from being locked up too. You were my jailer, and let me just note that you sucked at it. You gave me men's body wash to clean my hair with."

"Sounds like me." I snorted and turned to pace again, my anxiety rising at the thought of being locked up again when

Knight was still out there not knowing who I was. "I'm guessing I changed over time."

A smile crept over my face as I remembered the way he used to look at me. "You cherished me. You used to kiss my forehead like I would shatter into a thousand pieces if you kissed it too hard. You were gentle when I needed you to be. And... a little less gentle when I needed you to be." My eyes flicked to him and back before I could see what expression he had after that.

"That also sounds like me," he said, almost teasingly. When I checked his eyes again, he had a look on his face that made me weak at the knees.

"You tease me and I will shamelessly make out with you until you like me again," I warned, turning so I couldn't see him and stepping across the green carpet.

"Stop that, you're going to rub the carpet raw."

"I have to pace, I'm nervous. If they put me under house arrest again then I can't find my other husband." I crossed my arms over my chest and turned again, looking up when Arthur sighed loudly.

"I'll be right back." He went inside Othello's office, leaving me alone to ruin the carpet with my worrying. He didn't return until at least ten minutes had passed and I'd resorted to chewing on my claws in addition to the pacing. Othello and Marie were with him this time.

"The Council has agreed to absolve your crime. You are free to go," Othello said with a triumphant smile I did not return.

Instead, I smiled at Arthur, certain he had done something to sway their decision. He was already warming up to me, he'd be mine in no time. "Arthur, you're free to leave whenever you choose to. I'm sure the Hunters will need you back."

Arthur refused to meet my hopeful stare, making my stomach drop in terror that maybe I hadn't succeeded in winning him over as well as I thought I had. We'd only been together for maybe an hour, and last time it had taken almost a year. Maybe if I showed him my boobs...

"I have some things to do, so I'll be leaving immediately," was his answer, and I almost burst out crying. Othello dismissed us and Arthur walked past me out of the waiting room, but I was up on my heels and following him until he stopped in the foyer. "You'd better pack fast if you want to come with me." I raced off to my rooms and didn't even bother changing out of my sports bra and yoga pants, just grabbed the bag I'd already packed and then I passed him still waiting in the foyer on my way to the kitchen where I grabbed one of the communal coolers and filled it to the brim with blood packs. I'd barely even stopped to breathe in case he left without me, but he was still there when I returned completely out of breath. He quirked an eyebrow at my frazzled state. "Your hair is messed up."

"Oh pssh. Let's go."

6

RELUCTANT WEREWOLF

I was completely beside myself with anxiety. Going from what the witches said, Knight was in Kansas, near where I would've met him in a week or two if I'd let everything progress the way it had before. Arthur only mildly complained when I stopped at a particular car dealership and found my Excalibur waiting for me, the small blue car that had carried me to safety in my escape from Arthur's clutches. Now I would've given anything to be *in* his clutches.

Naturally, I bought it, and unfortunately had to pay them to send it back to the Order because it wouldn't fit everyone, providing we convinced Knight to come back with us. I had another car in mind for picking him up. We continued driving until we reached the second car dealership right outside of Kansas, and we bought the Impala that Knight had made me buy, the one he never stopped drooling over like it was a pair of breasts.

Before we stopped anywhere after reaching the Kansas state line, I texted the witch Isabelle from the number she gave me, and she confirmed the town Knight was in, which conveniently was the one we were about to enter. I pulled into the small city and I could barely focus on the road or the speed limit as I looked around for the coordinates Isabelle had given me that turned out to be the nearby state park, more specifically the public showers. After using my senses to check around for humans and finding none nearby, Arthur walked into the men's showers with me right behind him.

"What are you doing, this is the men's room," he hissed at me, pushing me away with his hand.

"Need I remind you, I've seen both of you naked," I whispered back, and ignored his protests, rounding the corner to a row of urinals on one side and a row of stalls on the other that both led to the showers. One of the showers was running and my steps slowed as I tried not to picture Knight naked under a steaming hot spray of water, with his tanned, muscled body and the five scratches on his stomach that always made him moan when I ran my fingers along them. "I should mention something else," I said quietly, but Arthur's senses were already picking up Knight's scent and his reaction was to grab my arm roughly and pull me in the opposite direction of where Knight was.

"Your other mate is a *fucking werewolf?*" Arthur accused, slamming me against the wall between two urinals. "When were you planning on telling me that you want to fuck the enemy?"

I pulled off from the wall and held my ground in the gross bathroom that smelled like sweaty piss. "He's not my enemy. He's never been my enemy. In my time, Lycans are my friends."

"I don't care what you did in your future," Arthur informed me, and then he pointed towards the showers with a grimace. "I'm never inviting that shit werewolf into anything, much less my bed."

"I never said you had to, and don't you *dare* talk about him like that!" I yelled back, and even though I wanted to sock him right in the face, I was two seconds from kissing him so hard he'd pass out, but the shower turned off and footsteps came closer to us.

"What's going on in here?" Knight stood in the tiled doorway holding a towel to his waist with his long, black hair dripping onto the floor.

Fuck it.

I ran across the bathroom and only stopped when I had my hands around his neck and was pressing his warm lips to mine in a kiss I would've died to have again. He passionately kissed me back, too in shock to do much else, until his nose kicked in and he shoved me away with disgust.

"The *fuck* are you doing? Get away from me, bloodsucker," he sneered, taking a step back. I tried to follow but

Arthur had stepped beside me and put a finger in my belt loop to keep me in place. Knight observed my companion, his anger and disgust sobering at the sight of a vampire that could kick his ass. "I don't want trouble. This isn't vampire territory, I'm free to be here."

I couldn't help myself, I took a step towards the love of my life and said the first thing I could think of to get him to listen while Arthur held me off with my belt loop. "Your sister Merrick is alive."

Knight's face went still and wary. "How do you know that? What game are you playing?"

I had to make him see. I couldn't go another moment with him looking at me like I was repulsive. "I'm not playing, I know everything about you. Your name is Jason Knight Trimble, you were born in Texas in 1842. You served in the Civil War and your mother died while you were gone." I kept trying to escape Arthur's finger until he pulled me up against his chest, locking me in by his arms, and tears rolled down my cheeks at the look on Knight's face from the sight of me, his enemy.

"You should get dressed," Arthur told him, dragging me back until we were out of the bathroom and I was sobbing against Arthur's arms in the warm sunlight. "Stop crying, he's not going to leave. You saw his face when you mentioned his sister. He wants to know what you know." Even though I was terrified Knight would just escape out the back door of the bathroom and leave us, Arthur was right, because a few minutes later Knight emerged from the facility holding his duffel bag and wearing his typical black shirt and blue jeans outfit. "I'm going to let you go, but don't try getting close to him again." I nodded and Arthur slowly released me.

"You two going to explain what you're doing here talking crazy shit about me?" Knight asked, watching us carefully. I opened my mouth several times but nothing came out, and Arthur pulled me back when I tried to bolt off to Knight's arms again.

"It's a little tough to explain," Arthur offered after I hadn't said anything for several minutes, mostly because I was caught between tears and needing at least one of them to hold me close. "Basically this woman here, Lisbeth is her name, claims she's from the future, one where you and I are her mated husbands."

Knight laughed, and the sight of it brought me from tears to a smile, even though he was laughing at me. "And you believed her?"

Arthur's shoulders went up in a subtle shrug. "She made a compelling argument. She knew something about me I've never said to anyone else. I'm sure she's got one for you as well."

Knight's look of expectation made me sorry I'd chosen this particular secret, but I let it out anyway. "Your dick grew bigger when you became a werewolf."

His eyes widened and he looked away to retain his

dignity in front of another man. "Wow. You're right, I've never told anyone that. Not exactly something you want women to know." Looking back to me, his brown eyes were turning my stomach over in a flurry of butterflies. "This future. We had sex?" I nodded, but his cold look in my direction made my smile droop. "I'd never touch a vampire like that."

Oh, but you did.

"You were mated with him too," I noted with a sniff, pointing to Arthur.

Confused, he scrunched his forehead up. "We —me and him— were lovers?"

"Well, yeah. You kissed a few times before it got a little... further than that."

"*Gross.*"

Arthur was immediately offended. "Gross? I can assure you my prowess is anything but gross."

"I don't even like boys," Knight said, which was an argument I'd heard before I found him kissing Arthur and it went out the window.

"You kissed that guy once during the civil war, remember that?"

"*Oh my god*, how many secrets did future me tell you?"

I leaned in closer and whispered, "All of them."

"Terrifying, isn't she?" Arthur said, making me swipe my foot at his leg that he easily deflected.

We hadn't won him over, but Knight slowly relaxed as

much as he could around us. "So what do you need me for, other than fucking, and I will note that is *not* on the table."

Pout.

"I need to save the world. And in order to do that, I need men I trust by my side. Meaning you, and Arthur here. Also a few others. Mostly you two."

"What do I get if I help you? Not that I will, because saving the world seems a bit of a stretch considering you're *vampires*," he sneered, making Arthur bristle at my side.

"Tell me again why I have to be polite to him?"

Instead of answering, I pulled out the paper in my pocket and carefully approached Knight to hold it out to him. "This is the location of your sister's coven. She's a vampire."

He looked disgusted but it passed quickly, his eyes darting to my hand holding the note. "And you'll tell me where she is if I help you?"

Watching him carefully, I took one step closer until he could take the note from me. "Your sister isn't a bargaining tool."

"I clearly failed to teach you the art of war," Arthur grumbled, but Knight took the note before I could change my mind, not that I would have.

"I'm under no obligation to help you, you know that, right?" he said as he stuffed the note into his pants pocket.

"I know." Being so close to him, his scent washed over me and I studied the planes of his face, the way his cheeks curved, the way his chin dipped, all parts of him I'd had so long to memorize.

He dropped his eyes, rubbing at his neck. "Don't look at me like that." My feet recoiled one step back and I turned my eyes down to my shoes. "How long were we together in your time?"

I answered without looking up because I feared my tears were about to return. "Sixty-six years."

His sharp intake of breath brought my eyes up to his waist, since the expression on my face was bothering him. "You stayed with me for that long?"

"I would've stayed with you forever." I took his silence as my cue to take more steps back until I could see Arthur on the side of my vision.

"So, what'll it be, werewolf?" Arthur asked him, and my pulse shot off with worry that this was all pointless and Knight would never agree to come with me. I felt sick right down in the depths of my belly, my saliva turning hot and salty when I swallowed.

"How will your kind not attack me if I agree to come with you?"

"One of us will have to bite you," Arthur answered.

Knight's nose wrinkled again in disgust, but he waved a hand at me. "I'd rather it be her." He kept the hand out, giving me permission to approach him, but he held it up when I was close. "Do *not* kiss me again."

I nodded and he clenched his fists when I stepped up, so close I could reach my hands up to take his massive shoulders in my small hands. I stood up on my tip toes as he leaned down, and being this close to him made me want to cry until I passed out.

My breath hit the skin on his neck and goosebumps formed on the surface. I almost didn't want to bite him because it would mean I'd have to go back to keeping my distance, and I wanted him in my arms for hours, but I had to hurry up before he changed his mind.

My fangs dropped down and I massaged the shoulder muscles under my hands so he would relax when I bit into his neck, marking him as mine, and I pulled a mouthful of his sweet, hardy blood, so rich and sweet it brought tears to my eyes, before his hands gently pushed me away. I quickly turned so he wouldn't see me licking my lips to get the last droplets of him off, but Arthur was free to see the turmoil on my face. Swallowing, I swiped my nose and sniffed, then I faced Knight again with a smile.

"I'll lead the way."

KNIGHT'S LOW, appreciative whistle at the Impala made my heart soar, until he climbed into the backseat and stopped talking. Arthur was also silent, leaving me unable to think about anything except touching Knight's skin again. I'd worked myself into a fever pitch by the time we stopped for the night, having driven all day to find Knight. As soon as we got inside our hotel room, I ran into the bathroom with my bag and curled up in the little closet where they kept the complimentary ironing board and all the towels.

My insides were a raging inferno, I was primed on the edge, and neither of them wanted me. We just needed time, that was all, but I'd let, if only for a second, the dread to come back in, the dread that was telling me this wouldn't work, and I'd save the world but at the cost of my happiness.

Stupid fucking witches, fucking everything up.

A door slammed and then there was a timid knock on the bathroom door.

"I've sent him for food," Arthur told me through the door. "You can come out." Only I couldn't move. I wanted to stay in the closet and just sleep there so I wouldn't have to see Knight looking at me like I was repulsive. The door opened and Arthur's shadow fell over me where I was sitting clutching my legs to my chest. "I don't know what to say to make this better."

"You know exactly how to make this better," I mumbled against my jeans. More tears were coming when he grabbed my arm and hauled me off the floor to stand in front of him, backing me up until I hit the wall of the closet. My body lit up again and the struggle on his face was overcome when he reached a clenched fist out and used it to grasp my hip. My face was a waterfall of tears, looking up at his icy features and longing to reach out for him.

He opened and closed his mouth several times until he finally decided what he was going to say to me.

"This is only sex. We're clear on that, right?"

Oh, god, yes.

In an instant, he was flush against me and I craned up to kiss his lips, needing, always needing more of him. He crushed my mouth with his, biting at my skin and holding me in place against him, and gods he was already so hard for me. I rocked my hips forward, running my belly along his length and he hissed against my lips, capturing them again as he shoved my pants down, helped me out of them, and lifted me up against the bathroom wall, cradling me in his powerful arms.

He released my lips, pulling his cock out of his pants and lining himself up with my entrance, and I leaned in to lick slowly up the scar on his cheek that he answered with a thrust deep inside me. I was already so wet, so ready, it wouldn't take long for me to explode against him, and I felt it rising as he started a rhythm against the wall, slamming my back into the concrete with every push of his cock.

Moaning against his shoulder, I nibbled on his ear and planted kisses on his scar before he roughly grabbed my hair and pulled my head back until my throat was exposed to him. He ran the tips of his fangs down it, making me so close to climax I was going to lose my mind. I got enough control of my head back to smash our lips together as I went over the edge and pulsed around his cock over and over.

He didn't stopped thrusting into me until my orgasm was over and he jerked his hips a few times, groaning against my lips as he came inside me. We slowed our movements and stood locked together, catching our breath, and I couldn't help myself.

I gently wiped at the drops of sweat on his forehead and kissed along his head, in every spot I could get to, then I held him to my breast and let myself believe he was my Arthur again.

HE LET me hold him close like that for a very long time, until we heard the hotel door open and he let me down gently on my feet, separating our bodies, and turned to put his still semi-hard cock back inside his pants before leaving the bathroom. I took a lengthy shower, trying to wrestle myself back into control before I went back to the man who didn't want me to look at him, and the one who confusingly just made love to me even though he still insisted he didn't want me, just like old times.

Getting out, I dried off, got dressed, and exited the bathroom, trying to keep my eyes on the floor as I dumped my backpack onto one of the beds and noticed Knight had brought a few pizzas for us. One was already empty and it had 'Knight's pizza' written in big letters on the lid, and the other one said 'Vampires only' that had a few slices missing, so I grabbed two and got onto the bed next to my bag.

"So you guys..." Knight said, gesturing with his piece of pizza. I flushed down to my toes and tried to focus on my food. Of course he could fucking smell it. No amount of scrubbing would erase our scents changing. Arthur didn't respond, just kept eating, and I did the same, but I could feel Knight's agitation over being ignored.

Did he care? I wanted so badly for him to care, but he'd told me to stop looking at him so I kept my eyes down and finished my pizza, tossing my used napkin into the bin beside Arthur's leg. Then I got underneath the comforter and pulled it over my head so I could fall asleep, a difficult feat with them both nearby but not snuggling against me. I tossed and turned for an hour while the two men ate more and sat in an uncomfortable silence that made me want to slap both of them.

Finally, Arthur sighed heavily and my comforter lifted up, then he slid in behind me and pulled me against his warmth, his large hand resting on my hip bone. He held said hip just enough away where our lower halves weren't touching.

"Don't get excited," Arthur murmured against my ear. "I just figured you needed one of us here so you can fall asleep."

"She's fine," Knight deflected, mouth full of pizza.

Arthur's hand curled on my skin and it sent a thrum of electricity throughout my body. "You obviously don't know what it's like to have someone in your bed for decades only for them to suddenly not be there." My hand reached up to rest on his, warning him to back off before I got angry, but also because I knew it was my pain that brought Arthur to me, because he understood it. It was what drew us together the first time.

I heard Knight getting into the other bed before shutting

the lights off. In the dark with my eyes adjusting, I rolled over to face Arthur's chest where I snuggled close and spoke to him in German, a language we both knew but Knight didn't.

"It's just sex, right?"

He answered by pulling me closer and tenderly kissing my forehead, like I would break into a thousand pieces if he pressed too hard.

7

BALTHAZAR IN THE MIX

I woke up the next morning like I usually did, with a burning hot erection pressed into my ass. I was back home and Arthur was there with me, so I eagerly rolled over and kissed his lips, snuggling into him and kissing down his neck. Once I was done with him, I'd find Knight and fuck him against the kitchen counters before everyone else in our home got up.

Everything was right again, everything was back to the way it should be.

"Where are the kids?" I asked him softly, and he instantly went frigid, pushing me away so he could look into my eyes.

"What are you talking about?"

Oh god. I wasn't back home. This nightmare was still real.

He watched the glow visibly leave my face until I was downtrodden and moved back to get off the bed. "No, you're not going to walk away. What did you mean by that?" He came at me like I was his prey, which wasn't going to help his plight, unless his goal was having me plastered all over him.

Thankfully, Knight was still asleep until my squeak as Arthur grabbed me woke him up. He snorted and sat up, rubbing his eyes. "What are you two doing? Go fuck somewhere else."

Arthur didn't flinch in his burning gaze on me, gripping my chin so I'd have to look up at him. "Tell me." I shook my head and he dropped his hands, searching my eyes for the answer that I refused to give him. "I won't fuck you again if you don't tell me."

My eyes narrowed at him and I tilted my chin in defiance as if I didn't care, when I totally did. "Fine." Stepping away from him, I roughly grabbed my bag and slung it over my shoulder, eyeing both men with a blank look. "I'll be in the car." I stomped out and wrenched the car door open, throwing my bag in before dumping myself into the front seat.

Fuck fuck *fuck*.

Why did I say that? Why did I believe, even for one second, that things had gone back to normal? Now I was on Arthur's radar, and he wouldn't rest until he found out what I wasn't telling him. I let out a string of curse words and got out of the car, walking away from the hotel until I'd reached a patch of trees, and I said the words to summon Balthazar to me.

He appeared with a wide smile, and leaned against the

tree in front of me like he'd been there all day. "Lovely to see you again, my dear. What's got your nose so red?"

Desperate to calm my raging emotions, my fingers curled and uncurled on my dress. "I need you to stay with me. Constantly. I know you hate it, but please. I'll beg if I have to. I need someone on my side, please."

The smile on his face faltered and he closed the distance between us before I could blink, wrapping me up in a lilac scented hug. I gripped the back of his jacket so hard I was sure it would tear and he pet at my hair to get me to relax.

"I'll do anything for you," he whispered, kissing my temple gently. The words comforted me, but I wondered if that was true. If I asked him to love me, could he? Could I, for that matter. He was certainly warm and comforting against my body.

I pulled my face away from his shoulder, tilting it so our cheeks brushed and our lips were so close I could've easily kissed his. Underneath the unrelenting turmoil inside me, I felt a magnetic pull to him, and that was something I couldn't keep denying.

This was why I'd kept him at a familial distance, because I knew it was there, waiting for me to discover. It wasn't love yet, but it could be if it had enough encouragement.

Like a simple kiss...

I couldn't risk it. If he pulled away, I'd have no one left. Cameron was set to leave any day now providing he didn't become a vampire again. Olivier didn't know about any of this, and my parents were half a world away. I longed for my aunt/step-mother Clara and her warm wisdom.

I pulled away from the Incubus in my arms and tucked some hair behind my ear. "Sorry," I mumbled, hoping I wasn't turning as pink as I felt. "Will you still stay with me?"

He started answering and had to clear his throat first. "Ye... Yes." A noise behind me made him look up, and I followed his eyes to see Arthur and Knight by the car, waiting for me. "I'm guessing one of them is who you were waiting for?" I nodded, watching them look over at us. "One smells like you, the other bears your mark. It seems you've been busy in my absence."

"All part of the plan," I joked absently, holding my hand out and he clasped it tightly. "Come on, we have a planet to save."

WITH BALTHAZAR IN THE MIX, he refused to let my other companions remain silent the rest of the way back home, but of course, his game was sex, and that was all he talked about.

He'd just finished regaling us about how he seduced a queen with very generous breasts, and it was even turning *me* on, when he stopped and tapped his hand against the front seat next to my leg.

"What was she like?" he asked, looking through the rearview mirror at the men in the backseat.

"Who?" I asked him, looking away from the road for a few seconds.

"You," he answered, still trying to catch Arthur's eye. "The stoic one made love to Lisbeth. I'm curious what it was like."

"What the *fuck*! You can't ask him that!" I was about to run us off the road from trying to keep Balthazar in my sights and make sure he stopped talking.

His teasing grin made me feel like a melting icicle. "I can, and I just did. Does the stoic one feel like answering?"

I groaned and resigned myself to this humiliation, keeping my eyes firmly on the road. "His name is Arthur."

What was Knight thinking about all this? Was he interested, or was he grossed out?

"It was pleasurable," Arthur answered, and I saw him looking out the window when I checked him in the rearview mirror. That was probably as good an answer as I'd ever get from him, even if I'd blown his mind.

"How tight? Like a little, or virgin tight," Balthazar probed, and I took one hand from the steering wheel to smack against him.

"I'm going to shove a burning pincer up your ass if you don't *shut up*."

When I was done, Arthur continued like we hadn't interrupted him. "Virgin tight."

"OH MY GOD," I shrieked. "Everyone in this car is going to shut their fucking mouths or I will find something to plug them with." They obliged, but I could tell Balthazar still had questions about my snatch that he was going to ask Arthur as soon as my back was turned. That is, if I didn't *kill him first*.

○┼──

AFTER A FEW HOURS, everyone had nodded off and I plugged my phone in to play some music. Music was one of the things I'd missed in the future. I turned on my favorite song and started singing along to the words, remembering all the times my version of Knight had sung it to me.

"I like this song," Knight said, startling me so I missed a few words.

I switched the song off and tried to focus on the road. "Sorry, I thought you were asleep." We rode in awkward silence until I saw him in the rearview looking at me. "I'm sorry about the sex stuff. I know you don't want to hear it. I know I'm repulsive." I curled and un-curled my fingers on the steering wheel, turning at the right spot so we pulled into town.

Knight shuffled in the backseat and looked away. "Every time I open my mouth, I think of more things to ask you about the life we shared in your time, but then I wonder if it even matters." It mattered to me. I wanted to say it, but I held it back. "How did you get me to trust you the first time?"

"A Lycan Alpha gave me his vampire teeth bracelet when I spared the life of a pup from his pack. You saw it and you swore to protect me."

"You don't have it this time," he noted.

86

"No. He offered it and this time I refused. I don't need a reward for doing the right thing. In my time, Lycans and vampires are allies. I will always treat them as such, no matter what time I'm in."

He was quiet for so long I looked in the rearview to make sure he hadn't gone to sleep.

"Your time sounds nice."

I settled back in my chair, a grin permanently fixed onto my face.

WE REACHED the castle at dinnertime and naturally we met opposition at the gate for having a werewolf with us, but my mark on him took precedence. The guards still accompanied us inside to Othello's office for his approval of the situation, and he greeted us with a grin that fell once he saw who was standing next to me. Or *what*, I should say.

"Get that *mongrel* out of here!" he barked, flicking his hands to the guards.

"I marked him, he belongs to me," I explained, watching with dread as Othello looked from me to Arthur to Knight.

He settled back on me and hissed, "This is utterly unorthodox. I do not condone mixing with worthless dogs."

I straightened my spine and stepped up to him, staring him down. "Don't talk about him like that."

His gaunt face twisted in shock and he moved back with

his scent stinking of fear. "Fine. I'll allow it. But I do not appreciate this insubordination, Lisbeth."

"I would like to petition a convening of the Council," Arthur said, exactly like we'd planned. Coming from me, the Council wouldn't listen, but Arthur was their top soldier for a reason. They trusted him. "In person this time. There's something I believe requires their attention."

Othello nodded, not for one second suspecting I was behind it. "Of course, Arthur. I will contact them and they'll be here in a few days. I hope whatever is wrong is not pertinent."

"Not yet," Arthur answered, and he motioned to me for us to leave. We piled out of Othello's office and waited for the soldiers to go back outside to guard the gate.

"God, I forgot what a weenie Othello is," I said, rolling my shoulders in disgust. "All I had to do was say one thing and he shrunk like a snow covered scrotum."

"I'm guessing he's not around where you came from?" Arthur asked, following me when I started walking.

I bobbed my head, avoiding the question. "Let's just say he did not last the night."

We went up the stairs and found our way to my rooms. My senses didn't detect Cameron nearby so I left the three men in my doorway and walked to Cameron's room, finding the door open and the room empty of his belongings.

He'd left me.

I tried to tell myself that this was a good thing, that it was better this way. He was safe from the horror of my life, and he'd never be killed for me. I told myself that over and over until Balthazar's hand touched my shoulder and I jumped away, hitting the doorframe with my shoulder.

"You umm…" I wiped my eyes and focused on the vanilla walls. "You guys should get something to eat. I'm going to take a shower." I hurried off so they couldn't see the tears getting worse and flooding out of my eyes at full speed.

I sobbed all through my shower, and by the time I was dried and dressed, I'd settled into that silent, depressive state that once encompassed me for weeks on end in these very rooms. Leaving my room wearing a simple dress, I saw Knight sitting alone on the couch playing a game on his phone. He looked up at me and I immediately dropped my gaze, pretending my arrangements needed straightening.

"You can look at me," he said, making me drop some of the flowers. "I know I said not to, but you look really depressing when you can't, so drink me in. All you want." Turning with a flower in my hand, I did just that. I stared at him for so long my legs started aching from lack of move-ment. I drank him in like a glass of thirst quenching water. His deep brown eyes, his long black hair, the dark tan of his perfect skin.

I loved him so much. I needed him like I needed air. I always had. I always would.

Until I dropped my eyes to wipe at my cheeks, he held my gaze no matter what passed across my face. I looked back up and he was studying me, watching me, with as much curiosity as caution.

"Damn it. How am I supposed to react when you look at me like that?"

"How am I looking at you?" I didn't think I was giving him a particular look, but then again I'd been staring at him like I had before, when he was mine.

"You look at me like I'm the only thing that's ever mattered to you. Like I'm the last thing you think of at night and the first thing you think of in the morning. Like you'll die if you can't see me anymore. Like I'm the reason your heart keeps beating."

Oh.

My fingers trembled so hard I dropped the flower onto the vanilla carpet. "I'd ask you to not talk to me like that if I can't touch you."

He got up from the couch and my breath left my lungs as he approached, stopping right in front of me, so close my breasts touched his stomach when I inhaled. Trembling, I held myself back, waiting as he lifted one hand up, running it through my hair, up my neck, resting on my chin that he used to pull me closer still so he could bend his head and hover right at my lips.

My brain turned to mush. The only thing that existed was Knight's lips and his warm breath on my face.

Finally, when I couldn't take it anymore, he leaned that extra distance and captured my lips with his. A groan escaped my throat and I threw my arms around his neck, curving my body against his, his passionate kisses scorching me from the inside out. Just as I was about to reach under his shirt, he pulled away, cutting me off from his warmth.

I felt stupid. Ridiculous. Unwanted. Emotions I never wanted to come from him.

My chest heaved, trying to catch my breath as he did the same. He ran a hand through his hair to push it out of his face, staring at everything except my eyes. I almost pushed into his head to see what he was thinking, but I was afraid of what I'd find.

He wanted me. I knew he did, but he didn't *want* to. My love for him was pushing him away when he'd always led me to believe he would've loved me no matter what.

I only had one option now. I had to abandon getting my family back and I had to focus on my mission of stopping Alistair. Once I did... Maybe I'd become a dolphin again, because if I didn't have the love of my husbands, my children, then I had nothing.

Clearing my throat, I smiled at him and pushed everything else deep down inside me. "I'm sorry, Knight. I've been pushing you and that wasn't fair. You don't have to kiss me again, it's fine."

Confused at my sudden mood switch, he looked at me like I was a crazy person. "Okay?"

Arthur and Balthazar walked in, letting me escape to my room where no one would tease me with beautiful kisses.

I SPENT the next few days alone in my room, feeling like I was in an endless torment, because I was. This was hell.

Accepting that I'd never get my babies back was worse than dying. No matter what I did, my heart refused to accept it. It longed for them, it longed for my lovers, it longed for my former life, but that life was gone, and I'd been chasing it ever since I came back. It was time to stop pining for what I couldn't regain.

Someone knocked on the door, and when I didn't answer, they (Arthur) walked in anyway, and the other footsteps meant we had an audience for whatever he was going to say.

"Are you done pouting?" he asked blankly.

"Fuck you," I threw over my shoulder from where I lay on my bed, looking out one of my windows where some birds were fluttering around because their lives were fabulous and perfect. *Fucking birds.*

"We've had a talk, all three of us," he continued. *God damn it.* "You're keeping something from us about the life we had in your time."

"Go away. I'm done talking about that. It's over. I'm never getting them... that back." Arthur's feet stomped across the room and he ripped the blanket off me, exposing me wearing short shorts and a tank top. I glared up at him. "You're lucky I don't sleep naked."

"*Tell us what you're hiding,*" he barked at me, so fiercely I winced.

"Please," Knight added, coming up beside Arthur, and that did me in.

Standing, I opened the drawer of my bureau and pulled out the necklace with four circles of hair, three black and one blonde. I held it up where all three could see it before clasping it around my neck and letting it settle between my breasts.

"Is that our hair?" Balthazar asked, looking at it curiously.

"No," I answered, staring up at Arthur, then I dropped my eyes and clasped the necklace front. "The witches took much more from me than the life we had together." I pointed to the top slot on the necklace. "Balthazar gave me Kitty." My fingers moved with each child to each bundle of hair. "Then Knight gave me Jason. Arthur gave me Dreya. And then Knight gave me Gwen."

I dropped both hands and felt the life draining out of me.

"The witches gave me a potion to get them back, but it won't happen now. Before you ask, it's because all three of you have to fall in love with me for the potion to work, and I know that's far too much to ask of you. Two of you hardly know me, and Balthazar is still in love with my grand-mother. So here." I unclasped the necklace and held it out for one of them to take. "I'm giving up. I won't get them back, and you don't have to help me. You can all go back to your lives and I'll save the world on my own. It was selfish of me to bring you here."

Knight took the necklace and I dropped my arm like it had turned to lead. "Would've been nice to know before now, considering you interrupted very important plans I made with a cheeseburger later."

"We won't promise to love you," Arthur informed me, and I felt even more shattered. "But the witches took you from us too. If they'd done nothing, we'd be with you, and our children would be here. I for one won't let that sacrifice fade away into nothing. And if we don't stop this Alistair then it will."

I loved him so much.

"We brought you some food, and the Council will be ready soon," Balthazar said. "I'd like to hear about my daughter."

My lip trembled and I shook my head. "No, I can't talk about them yet, but... I can show you." I put my hands out to them. "You have to touch me." They all approached without another word, but Arthur slipped his hand around my waist first.

"Anything to get our hands on you," he grunted, the most humor I'd seen on him in this timeline, and it brought a smile to my face even though I was broken inside. Knight put his hand on my shoulder while Balthazar clasped my fingers with his.

Using the last of my blood reserves, I opened up their minds and put us down in a field next to our home. Knight recognized it immediately as his childhood home, but he was side-swiped by a tiny Gwen running past him, trying desperately to escape Jason as he chased her around the yard. Kitty stood at the picnic table setting up for lunch while Dreya sat on the front steps crocheting Gwen a little yarn hat.

The sight of my babies had me doubled over, and I felt

someone pull me close to them outside our heads in the real world to steady me.

"Where are we?" Arthur asked, his eyes fixed on Dreya's movements, a hint of a smile pulling on his lips when she grinned at her siblings' antics.

"This was our home. This is a memory from two years ago," I explained, so weakened by the pain inside that I could barely keep the illusion up.

The other Knight, Arthur, and myself walked out of the front door, with Arthur holding one of her hands while Knight swept her up in a passionate kiss that all the children made faces over.

"*Mooom*, we're about to eat. That's *grossss*," Gwen blurted out from her big brother's arms once he'd finally caught her.

The other me laughed against Knight's lips and kissed him again just for good measure before Arthur took her away only to kiss her so deeply it took her breath away.

The stoic Kitty approached them and smiled one of her rare smiles. "Happy birthday, Mom." The other three children echoed her sentiment, along with my husbands who continued kissing the other me even with the kids complaining.

That day had been heaven. A party with my babies. A night of passion with my lovers. I could've never asked for more.

My strength waned and the image broke as my knees gave out. I was in Knight's arms, he'd been the one to keep me from breaking.

There was no help now. That day was gone forever. They were too.

Knight picked me up and carried me to the living room where they'd set up a tray on the coffee table with my lunch and a bag of blood I desperately needed. I reached for it with shaking hands and Arthur quickly picked it up, pierced it with a straw and handed it to me. Taking long pulls of it, I tried not to gag and finished it as fast as possible, tossing it onto the coffee table. The blood flowed through me and refreshed my powers, but it did little for the deep ache in my chest. I tried to stand but Knight's hand tugged on mine so I'd say seated.

"You need to eat," he urged, but I pulled back until he let me up.

"No, I have to go save the fucking world. It needs everything from me again, and I'm going to fuck it in the ass right back so it knows not to mess with Lisbeth fucking Bathory again."

"Bathory?" Arthur instantly asked, because that was the important part.

"Put your big boy pants on. We're about to fuck all the shit up."

8

THE FUTURE HATES ME

I marched out of my room with my three men on my tail, very aware I hadn't showered in days and I was wearing pajamas. My hair was probably messed up, and there was no telling how rank my breath had become.

I didn't care. I was done crying, I was done taking this lightly.

We didn't stop until we were outside of the bigger drawing-room doors, ready to bust them wide open by ripping on the handles until the room was exposed and I could see that stupid giant desk they'd used in my time.

Without waiting for an invitation, I marched up as they were still discussing what they were going to have for dinner. Typical.

"Yo," I said with a wave at them, automatically looking to Castilla, the only one on the Council who wasn't a moron.

"We're here. Can we do the thing?" Arthur growled next to me and I expected an ear flick, but he chose not to punish me. Yet.

Othello looked prim and proper, all the giddy crush gone from his face. "I've informed them about your insubordination of bringing a werewolf into our house."

Nark.

"We can begin," Castilla told him, sitting down while the other Council members did the same. "Arthur, you brought us here because you received intelligence about a threat to us."

"Correct. Lisbeth here was the one who told me about a vampire named Alistair that is rallying an army against us."

"She hardly seems credible," Estinien grumped, giving me an unimpressed once over. "I'm still confused as to why you vouched for her at her trial, Arthur. You don't seem the type to put your faith in someone as simple as her."

The *fuck* did you just say?

"You know what, fuck this." I stepped up to the desk as Estinien griped about my language so I shot him the finger. "Everyone put a hand on me. I have something to show you." Castilla was the first to do so, with everyone following suit, getting up from their seats to lay a hand on me somewhere. I felt Arthur, Knight, and Balthazar get in the mix, standing behind me in case I faltered again.

It took all of my strength to connect the minds of so many I hadn't drunk from, but I'd worked on my abilities for years to do just that. I showed them all the highlights of my timeline.

Me saving Simon. Running from Arthur. Meeting Knight. Falling in love with him. Being captured. My endless trial. Becoming the leader of my Order. The hidden feelings I had for Arthur. Having Kitty. Finding my parents. Leading us to victory against the turned army. Having Jason. Alistair destroying the world. Having Dreya. Finding Salvation. Losing Arthur. Losing Cameron and Merrick. Hendrix's cruelty. Kitty and Arthur returning to me. Defeating Hendrix. Having Gwen.

And then that last day, when Selene found me and told me she was the last witch alive and that I had to go back in time to prevent Alistair from destroying everything, and seeing Gwen and Knight's face for the last time as they ran towards me before I disappeared into blackness, as I did again in the drawing-room, falling back into Knight's arms and passing out.

WHEN I CAME TO, I was in my bed with an IV in my arm connected to several blood bags on a metal IV stand beside me. My head was spinning as I sat up and I clutched it with a groan.

"Easy, take it easy," someone, Knight, said to my right. His hands came up and he pressed me back against the pillows.

"You stupid woman, you drained yourself completely,"

Arthur chastised on my other side. "You've been asleep for days." He said that, but what I heard was he'd been beside himself with worry over me. "You're lucky you woke up at all."

"Mmm," I buzzed, taking his hand and putting it to my lips. "There's no way I wouldn't wake up with you taking care of me, you big icicle." I kissed his scarred knuckles, one after the other. "I love you." Another dizzy spell hit me when I flipped my head over to Knight and I reached out for his hand too that I gently kissed. "And I love you. I know you don't want me to. But I do."

"What about me?" Balthazar was by my feet, and I smiled at him in my haze.

"I've always loved you, silly." The effort to focus was more than I had in me, but I managed to look up at Arthur. "What happened with the Council? Did they decide not to care?

"Yes."

I groaned and squeezed his hand. "Stupid cautious fucks. They almost got us killed several times because they're all morons."

"They were pretty impressed with your powers, though," Knight offered, lacing his fingers with mine.

Balthazar clutched my foot, massaging the sole gently. "I quite enjoyed the movie of your life. I noticed you didn't show us fucking. What was it like?"

I giggled and my head throbbed. "It was pretty awesome. But my first time with Knight was much better." I leaned into his hand and snuggled it, happy to have his scent enveloping me in my sleepy state.

"Humph," Balthazar grumped. "There's no way he was better than me. I'm an *Incubus*."

"Blah blah blah, your dick is mind blowing, we know," I mumbled, and drifted off to sleep against Knight's fingers.

UNAWARE HOW LONG I'D slept again, I woke up for a second time in my bed, this time missing the IV, but I still had Knight's hand against my cheek.

He was sitting beside me, playing on his phone with his free hand, and he looked down at me when I stirred. "Ahh, finally. You have no idea how hard it is to play a racing game with one hand."

I groaned from the heavy feeling in my head and stretched out with a yawn. "I'm sure there are other things you can do one handed."

He sniggered under his breath, fully engrossed in his game with both hands on the screen now. "Touché."

I was just about to go to the bathroom and clean up when my phone rang on my nightstand. I picked it up and it was a number I didn't recognize. "Hello?"

"Hello, is this Lisbeth?" It was a woman's voice, and there was something about it I couldn't quite place. "Look, this might be a little weird, but we've never met. I mean, I've never met *you*. You've met me."

Then it hit me. "Sara?"

"Bingo! Listen, I've been having some visions about you and I think you should come visit. You can bring your three lovers with you."

I glanced back at Knight, still playing his game. "They're not... my lovers." He looked up at me in confusion and I waved a hand for him to continue playing.

"Oh, I understand," she chimed in. "That's one of the things we have to discuss. I'm also gonna need you to leave immediately. I know you're tired, but you have to. It's imperative. Capiche?"

"Umm, sure?"

"Awesome! I'll put out a roast. See you soon!"

She hung up and the line went dead, leaving me staring at my phone with that face I always made when I was around Sara, the one that said I had no idea what she was doing, because I didn't.

"Who was that?" Knight asked me, watching me slip my phone into my pajama shorts.

"A friend. She's psychic. She wants us to come see her. Like. Now." I looked around for my bag and found it tossed into the corner amongst several pairs of men's shoes and their respective belongings. I grabbed the shoes and bag I knew belonged to Knight and put them on the foot of the bed. "I wasn't kidding. Let's go." He hopped up and started lacing his shoes as I grabbed a change of clothes and put on a clean pair of jeans with a plain tee in the bathroom, then I brought my bag and a pair of boots with me into the living room where Arthur and Balthazar were also getting ready, having no doubt listened in.

"A psychic, huh?" Arthur asked, his head bent over his shoes.

"I've learned to listen to her. Sorry if that disrupts our plans."

Balthazar was tapping his cane against his leg. "We don't have plans anymore, not after the Council voted on being dumb asses. We'll do whatever you say."

Grinning, I strummed my fingers on my backpack strap. "Where's Cameron?" I asked Arthur once he was up. With Cameron's room empty, I knew Arthur would know where he went.

"Olivier's got him. I clued her in on everything. She's taking him and Renard on a trip to keep them safe, just in case." My lungs released a sigh of relief that Cameron hadn't abandoned me, and because Arthur had thought of it before I had to ask him. Good old Arthur. Always anticipating my needs.

With all of us ready, we headed out down to the parking garage and piled into the Impala, Knight in the front seat with me this time. I still wasn't letting anyone else drive, but he was the only one willing to choose the music on my phone so we didn't ride in silence again.

James' town was further away than the one we'd found Knight in, so we had to stop for the night eventually, but first we needed to eat. I rolled into a diner that looked like it belonged on the set of Supernatural, one where Dean shoveled pie into his mouth while he flirted with the waitress and Sam ate a modest salad at his computer.

We got out and went inside. Balthazar was eyeing the place like he was certain just looking at it would make him ill.

"They'd better have confections," he complained in a whisper.

I navigated to a booth and Balthazar scooted to the inside of one side while I sat next to him with our two companions across from us. A waitress approached us, holding menus and rolled up silverware in paper napkins.

"Welcome to Salty Steve's. Something to drink?"

Knight put his hand up when she started passing out the menus. "She's ordering for us." I tilted my head in confusion. "I want to see what you think we'd like."

I wiggled my fingers until the waitress handed me a menu that I scanned just enough to memorize what was on there before handing it back. "The long haired gentleman will have a soda, a triple cheeseburger with fries, a rare steak, and half of an apple pie. The icy hot one will have hot coffee with a BLT sandwich and a bowl of grapes. And the sex god to my right will have the other half of the apple pie with a can of whipped cream and some hot tea." Knight's wide grin had me so flustered I almost couldn't get all of the order out without fumbling over my words.

"And you?" the waitress asked me when she'd written it all out.

"Hot tea, and the burrito meal. No, make it the platter."

TIME OF THE ANCIENTS NSFW SPECIAL EDITION

She left, leaving me to stare at Knight's smile for as long as I wanted.

"I'd say she passed any test you had in mind for that," Arthur noted, unrolling his silverware.

"Never pegged you for a salad guy," Knight retorted with a smirk to the vampire.

"You've definitely been pegged though," I told him, and had to dodge the crumpled up napkin Knight threw at me.

Arthur was quick to add, "I'm sure he's had his salad tossed too." I erupted in giggles and held out a high five for him that he barely looked up at. "Nope."

"Damn it, you're the same in every timeline."

As we were the only customers this late at night, our food was ready in what felt like mere minutes and we all made space on the table for Knight's three plates. My large plate was loaded with four burritos on it, surrounded by a lake of beans and rice. I lifted two of the burritos and put them beside Knight's cheeseburger. He looked at them and up at me, his mouth already full of French fries.

"Sorry," I said, bringing my hands back to my plate. "I forgot to get you some. I know you love them." He continued staring at me, confused at my actions again.

Arthur popped a grape into his mouth and chewed it as he surveyed my meal. "Where's mine?" I'd never remembered him liking them, but I lifted one of mine without a thought and started bringing it to his plate, only for him to stop me mid-journey across the table. "I was joking. I just wanted to see if you'd give me one."

"Ass," I grumped, and cut a bite of my burrito after putting it back on my plate, swirled it in the beans, and popped it into my mouth. It tasted so good, almost as good as the burritos Knight used to make me.

"You'd give up all your food for us, wouldn't you?" Arthur observed with another grape in his mouth.

I met his eyes and then Knight's before looking back down at my plate. "Maybe." Before I could blink, Knight had handed me his pie, Arthur his bowl of partially eaten grapes, and Balthazar his can of whipped cream, but not before putting some on his half of the pie. I got my fork and took a generous bite of Knight's pie portion. "Better stop spoiling me, I might get the wrong idea," I said around the savory fruit and crust.

Or the right one.

I heard the thought with my powers, but it was so faint I couldn't tell which one of them had said it. They were all busy eating and weren't looking at me.

Maybe I'd imagined it.

WE GOT a hotel room with two big beds and we went to sleep with full bellies, Balthazar in my bed and Knight sharing the other with Arthur. I would've preferred being sandwiched between my husbands like I used to, but no, they were sleeping in the same bed so there was no telling how long it would be until they started making out without me. As long as I got to watch.

I woke up with someone snuggled into my ass, his hand slowly sneaking up to my breast where he stopped, and I was too groggy to even care. I took the hand and put it right on my boob, then I realized it was Balthazar and almost jumped away from him.

"Morning," he whispered, his chin on my bare shoulder where my shirt had drooped. "Been awhile since I've touched a breast. It's nicer than I remembered." His fingers slowly squeezed and I gasped audibly, pulling his hand away before he could do more.

I rolled over to face him just in case he got handsy again. His black hair was mussy and it curtained his pink face, falling over one eye. I pushed it out of the way so I could see both blue globes clearly, and he kissed my wrist when it was close enough to his lips. This was nice, being this close to him. I was able to notice all the dips and curves of his face, the way they looked chiseled by stone. He really was a beautiful man.

"You think I'm beautiful?" he asked, smiling in his teasing way.

I'd spoken aloud, as I did sometimes when I was distracted, and I blushed under his smile. "Duh. You're a sex god."

His deft fingers danced up my arm. "Did I use my powers on you?"

I gulped and stared at the skin of his neck that was

uncovered by the top button of his shirt being undone. "Ye... yes." I cleared my throat.

His blue eyes studied me, making flames burn across my skin where they landed. "I can see exactly how you want to be taken."

Oh, Jesus. I was going to dissolve into a puddle of need again if he didn't stop talking.

I moved like a blur, taking his neck in my hand and pressing his lips to mine, and *god*, it was just as good as the first time, except I wasn't desperate to feel wanted now, desperate to feel loved. I just wanted him, like I wanted Knight and Arthur. Every twist of his mouth was like a pulse through me, a wave of pleasure as powerful as if he was inside me.

He rolled us over until he was on top of me, kissing along the seam of my lips and thrusting his tongue into my mouth. I felt something between my legs with each push of his tongue against mine, a phantom sensation like he was fucking me with his cock, even though our clothes were still on. It felt so good, I had to moan loudly against his mouth and he smothered it with another thrust of his tongue.

The more we kissed, the deeper the sensation went, making my pleasure rise until I was sure I would climax without him touching me. When I was certain I couldn't take it anymore, his hand slipped beneath my shorts and he flicked my clitoris one time making me cry out, starting an orgasm that ripped through me like lightning. He kept our lips together to muffle my moans as much as possible as I came down, gasping in air like a dying man when he let me up to breathe.

"Balthazar powers sample *deux*," he whispered against my swollen lips. With the last dredges of my climax running through me, I claimed his mouth again, savoring the lilac taste of him that was hitting me anew, but it was somehow different now.

Turning my head to the side, I was pleased to see our companions were still asleep, and I knew they weren't faking with a quick check inside their heads. Balthazar kissed at the exposed skin on my neck and I moaned, so ready for round two, but we had to get up and keep moving.

Well. Maybe after more kisses.

WE MADE IT TO JAMES' town in one piece, which was hard to do when Balthazar kept turning his powers on me so I constantly felt like he was resting his hands on my breasts, and every so often would flick the nipples. Christ, this was the best and the worst at the same time. If I hadn't been driving, I'd have been perfectly fine with it, especially if those hands went south, but I was the only one who knew where we were going.

I eventually pulled up to Sara's B&B as coiled as a spring and jumped out of the car to try and cool off before we went inside, but the front door opened and Sara waltzed out with her pink tipped braids, holding a bowl of chickpea batter against her generous body.

"Lisbeth!" she called, waving her spoon and dropping batter onto the sidewalk. "Oh, your lovers are much cuter in person. And with their clothes on."

"*What?*" Knight stammered.

"Just go with it," I whispered to him, and followed Sara into her inn, dodging drops of batter on the way. We entered the same hippie red lobby I remembered with her artwork strewn about and hung on the wall. Someone came out of the kitchen licking his fingers and smiling at us, waving happily.

Fuck.

I flinched back at the sight of James, the vampire that had held me captive here with his bite, controlling my every movement. Even though none of them knew about it, my reaction had Arthur stepping in front of me to keep me safe from the guy who was dipping his fingers into Sara's bowl and licking them again.

Grossssss.

"He won't hurt you, Lisbeth. He's sobered up now, I promise," Sara assured me, trying to bend so she could see me from behind Arthur's imposing frame.

"What'd he do to you in your time?" Knight asked, also standing close to me.

I made sure I had contact with all three of my men as I showed them a clip of my time as James' slave, making sure to note how Knight had taken care of me during it. I shut the image off and stepped back.

"That."

Knight thrust his chin in a challenge at James. "You touch her and you're dead."

Be still, my heart.

Sara handed James the rest of the batter that he started devouring with his fingers. "Calm down, I said he's harmless. He's never going to do that to her in this time."

I stepped out of my man curtain and approached the batter eating James, standing as close to him as I could without wanting to vomit. "You touch me again and you won't have to worry about the gigantic walls of muscle behind me. I'll end you myself."

He barely reacted, seeming as if whatever Sara did to him had turned him into a docile puppy. "You're scary." He leaned into me and I bent back, grimacing. "I like it."

Sara pat his shoulder lovingly and they shared a gross look. "James, love, could you entertain the men in the sitting room while Lisbeth and I talk?" He nodded and walked away with the bowl in his arms, my men dutifully following him behind some red curtains to the sitting room on the other side of the lobby. "Ahh, that's better. Hard to think with all that delicious in front of me. I don't know how you can focus on anything."

"It's definitely an effort," I noted, grinning at my old friend. "I've missed you. It's been a long time."

She motioned for me to follow her into the kitchen where she'd laid out several plates of chickpea pancakes layered with salsa, avocado slices, and some hummus. "Imagine my surprise waking up one day somehow knowing you were here, not even knowing who *you* were, and through all the little tidbits my head was sending me, one of them was I'd died at some point and you never saw James or my son again."

"You got really sick and you refused to let him or me turn you," I explained, sitting at the table as she sat across from me. "It was before the apocalypse happened. We were there when you died, and then James and Drake disappeared." I reached out for her hand, the sadness of the memory overwhelming me. "I'm glad you're fine again."

She gave me a consoling pat on my hand and served me a plate of pancakes. "You've lost more than just me along the way. I don't expect you to mourn me as long as you can throw me, not compared to losing the man you called brother, losing your freedom, losing the man you love."

While that was all true, I'd still missed her.

"Well, since everything is out in the open, there's another thing I should tell you about me." I waited and she held out her hand until a crack of lightning went from her pinkie to her thumb. I should've been surprised, honestly, but I wasn't, especially when she continued. "I'm a witch. I went to Highborn when I was a teenager. You sensed the power inside me because I'm not human. You've become a total badass with your abilities too, by the way. You didn't have these powers at all when we met before."

Grinning, I sliced into my pancakes with a fork and dipped them in the hummus before taking a bite. "I've had some time to practice."

She got up and rummaged in the teal cabinets, looking for something. "Where did I leave... Can never find the darned thing when I need it." She bent to look under the sink and then slid open the lid on her metal bread keeper. "Ahh, there it is."

Reaching inside, she produced a glass orb with smoke swirling inside. "Full disclosure, I was kicked out of Highborn because my magic is too chaotic, too hard to control. But I can still use this." She walked back to the table and set the orb down where it stayed still even though there was nothing underneath it to keep it in place. "What we'll see might be a bit cryptic, but we'll try to figure it out together. Hands on the orb, please."

The orb felt like touching a beating heart full of warmth and life, but also cold and unfeeling at the same time. She put her hands over mine and spoke some words that resembled the ones Headmaster Cauldron had used for his magic. The smoke in the orb shot up from the glass and swirled around us, enveloping us in its tumultuous cloud.

We weren't in the kitchen anymore, I felt more like I was in a movie theater, watching something play out in front of me. Sara's powers only let us observe, whereas mine let me become part of the images.

Playing in front of me was... basically an orgy. Me with all three of the men I loved, naked and having a good time, it seemed. If we weren't mid-vision, I knew Sara would've given me a high five.

We were finding my parents, and the journal I'd gotten from the future was in Anastasia's hands.

I was leading a march of Lycans and vampires to defeat Alistair, but the last image stopped me cold.

Knight was lying on the ground, dead.

9

REFUSAL NO MORE

*N*o. No no no. This couldn't happen. This wasn't the future. I couldn't have been brought back only to lose him.

I pulled myself from the orb and backed away from the table, my chair falling onto the floor as a wave of nausea overcame me. "Tell me," I said as calmly as I could muster, but it wasn't calm at all. "Tell me how to prevent that. I don't want him to die, please, Sara."

She stood, grimly holding the orb in her hands. "If you send him away, you won't get your children back."

Hot, burning tears stung my eyes and I shook my head at her, denying that this was real. "If he stays, he dies. I'd rather die myself than let that happen, I don't care about anything else."

"Lisbeth, you can't change what I saw."

"I won't let him die," I shouted, my throat warbling, and I turned to run out of the room, across the lobby, right to the curtains that I thrust aside to reveal James standing with his gross batter, Knight and Arthur on the couch talking about something on their phones, and Balthazar sipping a glass of wine he somehow had. I went straight to Knight and wrenched him up from the couch, pushing him until he was near the doorway. "Get out. I don't want you here." The words were poison in my mouth, running through my body like cancer.

He looked as much in turmoil as I was, confused by my sudden outburst. "What are you talking about?"

"I said *get out*. We don't want you here. You're..." I had to force myself to swallow before the word would come out. "...*repulsive*." It wasn't working on him, I'd made such headway with him that he didn't believe me, so I had to try harder. I had to say something that was the biggest lie I could think of. "I only stayed with you in my timeline because Arthur didn't want me. You were a replacement. I never wanted to be with you." I hoped my face didn't betray how false every word I said was, but Knight's confusion went away.

"You don't mean any of that," he reasoned, a slight glisten of tears forming in the corners of his eyes.

I sucked in a breath and tried to keep my chin from trembling. "I do. Now get out. I should've never brought you into this. We don't need you. I don't need you."

Lies. All lies.

Arthur's hand slid onto my arm and stayed when I tried to shake it off. "Lisbeth, stop it."

"Not until he leaves," I insisted, weakly shaking my arm to get him to let me go. "He has to leave."

"Balthazar, take her upstairs," Arthur ordered, only letting me free when Balthazar had his hands on my other wrist. I wrenched away and ran out, bumping Knight's shoulder as I went, and I didn't stop until I was inside the room I'd had before, curled up in the Steampunk bathroom.

This was all my fault. I was going to lose him again. He'd almost died before because of me, and now he was going to die again, and it was all my fault.

Sobs racked my chest so hard I felt like all of my ribs were broken. Every wave of sadness sent me more into the corner until I was bent at an uncomfortable angle and my phlegm was getting all over the wall where I'd rubbed my face against it.

If Knight left, I wouldn't get my children back, but he would live. He had to live. I couldn't lose him again, I wouldn't have anything left. I'd rather die.

The bathroom door opened but my eyes were useless and my senses were preoccupied with life altering sobs.

"Tell me something," the person said, and I knew it was Knight without seeing him.

I turned my wet face to him, scowling. "I told you to go away."

He ignored me, walking closer to me until he was

covering me with his shadow. "You'd rather give up getting our kids back than let me die?"

"You're *everything* to me. They wouldn't want you to die for them. They never would've wanted that."

"That's not what you said just now."

I glared at him even though I couldn't make out his features. "I fucking lied, like that wasn't *fucking* obvious. I almost lost you before and it destroyed me. I won't go through that again." Wiping my tears did nothing, so I settled for resting my chin on my knees. "Do you know what the last thing I said to you was?" He didn't know, of course, so he waited for me to tell him. "I said, *'I love you, but stick it up your ass.'* That's such a perfect send-off for the love of my life."

He sighed and held a hand out to me. "Stand up."

I curled my hands around my knees tightly and looked down at the floor. "No. Why aren't you gone yet?"

Grunting, he bent and lifted me up like I weighed nothing, holding me out in front of him when I refused to put my feet on the ground. "Because I fucking love you, you moron."

He pushed me against the wall and crushed my lips in a heady kiss. I didn't want to respond, but fuck, I couldn't help myself. I whined, bringing my hands up to tunnel through his long hair, deepening the kiss and flooding my body with a warmth that settled between my thighs. He responded with a growl, smelling how much I wanted him, and roughly brought my hips against his, pressing me against his hard length. I pulled away from his mouth and kept our eyes locked as I reached one hand down to trail along the front of his pants, making him gasp deep in his throat.

Regrettably, he stepped back, and I whined again until he took my hand and led me out of the bathroom where Arthur and Balthazar were waiting for us in the small bedroom. Knight stepped away from me until all three of them were in my slightly blurry sight.

"We've all talked again," he started, and squeezed my hand when I squinted in disbelief that they were doing this to me exactly like they had in my time, making choices without talking to me first. "The potion the witches gave you said that all three of us had to fall in love with you. But even so, you never tried to make us love you in order to get our children back. You just wanted us to love you again."

I scoffed and wiped at the drops on my chin. "I'm not quite that unselfish."

"You are," Arthur insisted firmly. "And I fell in love with you the first moment I saw you on that sparring mat, when you walked up and weren't afraid of me for one second. Even Olivier is afraid of me, but you aren't. You've never been. And god, you're the strongest woman I've ever met." Even through my tears, that made me smile, because it was so close to what he'd said to me when we were together in my time. "It would be my honor to protect you with my life for as long as I live."

I managed a small laugh that puffed out a few tears from my mouth. "You're so sappy, that's gross."

"Don't forget me," Balthazar chimed in. He'd lost the

cane, his jacket, cravat, and vest, and the top few buttons of his shirt were undone. I'd never seen him look so casual. So relaxed. "You were right with what you said before. I only loved you because of the Countess, because I promised to watch over you when she died. I confused my love for you with my love for her, but you're not her. You're different, you're stronger than she ever was. She would've never sacrificed her happiness for me. I know we didn't end up together in your future, but now the thought of not having you is maddening. I need to be by your side, if you'll have me." He stopped, his Adam's apple bobbing as he swallowed hard. "I love you, Lisbeth. Not as family. As a woman. As you."

With their speech done, Knight stepped closer to me, his hand running up the length of my arm, making my body tingle all over.

"You know exactly how to please us. If you'll let us, we'd like to learn how to please you."

I clutched him to me, my salty tears mixing with our kiss when our lips came together. With Knight's arm around me, I turned to Arthur who came up and kissed me hard, demanding I pay attention him, but still allowing Knight to keep his arm around me.

Then I turned to Balthazar who was waiting, as he always had been, and he approached me cautiously, sliding his hand up mine until he was so close our breath mingled, and we kissed passionately, finally together without hesitation.

They surrounded me and I smiled up at Arthur. "I'm used to juggling two men. Three is a little different."

He grinned at me and reached back to let my hair down from the braid I'd put it in. "Knight, take her to the bed."

I was lifted by his arms before I could react and he put me down beside the mattress, lifting my shirt off, tossing it away. Before he reached for my pants, he bent and suckled one of my nipples into his hot mouth and I rubbed against him like a cat in heat. With Knight distracted against my breasts, Arthur reached in between us and unzipped my jeans, thumbing his way into my panties and pulling them both to the floor, leaving me naked in front of all three of them for the first time in this timeline. Knight moved away from my breasts as they took me in and I felt like a piece of priceless art from the looks on their faces.

With them momentarily stunned, I hopped up onto the bed and wrapped my bare legs around Knight's waist, pulling him to me by his shirt until I could capture his lips with mine. Finally, I was able to remove his shirt, toss it, and run my hands along the pinkened scars on his stomach, and he moaned just as I knew he would.

He growled at me and took my hands away from his chest. "Not playing fair. This is our turn." I smiled, remembering him saying similar words to me when we first became lovers. He was becoming my Knight again, and god I needed him so badly, I ached for him.

I didn't care that they'd planned exactly how to please me, I wanted him inside me. My hands wiggled out of his so I could reached for his pants zipper, and he motioned to Arthur who was now freshly naked. Arthur came up behind me on the bed, took my wrists and slid me across the comforter until my head was between his legs and my wrists were spread, pinned by Arthur's hands so I was helpless beneath him.

My pulse sped up, my chest heaved in anticipation when I heard Knight's pants falling and he climbed up me until his face was level with my belly button. I knew the look on his face well, he was going to devour me and I couldn't stop it even if I wanted to. Keeping eye contact with me, he trailed his chin down my stomach until it disappeared between my legs, and he used his hands to spread me open, the cold air hitting the dripping heat waiting for him. My legs started trembling underneath his hands, so ready, so on edge.

An also naked Balthazar leaned in over Arthur's arm and kissed me possessively as he tweaked one of my nipples. "You're loving this so much, you're going to come the instant he touches your clit with his tongue," he teased against my lips. Damn him. "Tell him what you want."

"Stop teasing me, you bas- fucking Christ, oh my god." Mid-complaint, Knight had reached his tongue out to flick my clitoris, and just as Balthazar predicted, I shot off like a rocket, climaxing so hard I writhed on the bed and Arthur struggled to keep me pinned. As I came down, chest heaving, Balthazar leaned back and sat next to me.

"Fuck her, Knight. She wants you."

I heaved and lifted myself up, pulling free from Arthur so I could meet Knight and drag him on top of me. He kissed me, spreading me wider so he could fit between my legs, and he reached a hand down between us to slowly slide inside me. I cried out in ecstasy, finally having him where I'd needed him all this time. It was so much better than I'd remembered, and as he started moving in and out, my toes were already curling and I could feel another orgasm building up without much effort, but I didn't want to yet, I wanted this to last as long as possible.

It was almost impossible to speak with this much pleasure filling me, but I reached out for Balthazar's hand. "Don't let me come again until he does." My words trailed off with a long moan, but he got the message, and I felt my body tensing up, still ready to climax but unable to.

Knight sat up, leaning over me, and he gripped my thighs as his thrusts sped up and he fucked me hard and fast, leaving me breathless and poised. Everything rose inside me, I was a wave that couldn't crash down, but I still craved more.

"God, you were right, Arthur," Knight huffed with his blinding pace. "She's so damn tight, I'm going to lose it." As lost as I was with pleasure, it didn't override my brain enough where I didn't see Arthur's hand timidly reaching out to my lover, and Knight took it, giving him a look I'd seen before.

Oh god. Fucking hell, yes.

I moaned loudly, but not from the sex, because Arthur leaned over me and kissed Knight on the lips with enough passion to melt the polar ice caps, as if he'd been waiting to do it since they first saw each other. It sent Knight over the edge with a surrendering groan against Arthur's mouth and he thrust his come inside me. With a kiss to my lips, Balthazar let me go and I came so hard I saw stars, squirting liquid all over the bed and all over us. It felt like I was having three orgasms at once, heightened by Arthur and Knight still making out above me.

"If you two are busy, I'd be happy to take her," Balthazar mentioned casually, trailing a hand over my heaving breast again.

Arthur broke from Knight's lips, giving him a look that definitely said they'd continue that later, and he met my eyes below him. "It's my turn, Incubus." My body thrummed in response, as if I hadn't already had two massive orgasms, and I sat up when he motioned for me to. He set himself up against the headboard and guided me to his lap, then he rubbed his cock against my slit and captured one of my nipples in his mouth, biting down when he shoved me down on his dick until he was completely inside me, balls deep. "Still so tight and wet," he mused against my nipple, using his hands to lift me up slightly so he could thrust into my wet cave. His other hand roughly grabbed a chunk of my hair and he held me in place, intent on taking exactly what he wanted from me. With his cock moving in and out like a piston, I was in erotic bliss. "Make her come, Balthazar."

I wasn't even close to an orgasm and I started to protest, but Balthazar had already obeyed and I was careening into climax, shuddering around Arthur's cock that didn't stop fucking me even for a second.

"Again."

"No, fuck—" He didn't listen, the Incubus just sent me into a second orgasm that had me squirming under Arthur's grip and I struggled to catch my breath with waves of pleasure making me whimper for mercy.

I would get none.

"Fuck, I need her again," Knight said, coming up behind me and kissing my bare shoulder. Arthur kept my eyes locked with his as Knight's cock probed my ass and slowly pushed inside. My eyes rolled back in ecstasy, sending a fresh stream of wet from where our bodies were joined.

"Looks like she likes being ass fucked," Arthur teased, pulling my head to his lips so he could kiss my neck.

"Damn it, I love it, please fuck me," I pleaded under my breath, gasping when Knight's cock started matching Arthur's tireless rhythm. Full to the brim, completely surrendered to them, my powers took over without me trying to use them. I was suddenly inside all of their heads and they were in mine.

"Fuck, what... fuck me harder," Knight breathed on my back. "Jesus, I can feel everything."

Arthur was dangerously close to coming with the added pleasure, and I reached between us to rub my clit a few times, knowing it would send him over the edge along with myself and Knight. We came at the same time, shooting, squirting, shuddering, until we fell in a heap against each other, utterly spent. Knight dragged us down onto the bed and we caught our breath with Balthazar at my feet, who still hadn't had his turn with me. He waited until we'd calmed down enough before he slowly tugged me until I was standing next to the bed with him behind me, pressing his hard cock against my ass.

His lips hovered over my ear, breathing onto the lobe and making me shiver against him. "I'm going to fuck you so hard while Arthur fucks Knight. You get to watch, but you can't touch them." Damn it to hell, I was about to die from pleasure. "You're going to come so many times, you won't be able to tell where one ends and another begins, until you beg me to stop."

His talk was making my pussy drip down my legs, I'd never been so turned on in my life, but even that was heightened when I watched Arthur kneeling between Knight's legs, kissing him roughly, passionately, and sliding his cock inside to start gently fucking my lover's ass. Knight moaned, running his hands to Arthur's nipples and making the vampire toss his head back with a groan.

When I was unable to stand it, Balthazar nudged my feet until they were spread enough for him to slide his cock inside my pussy. His fucking was as slow as Arthur's, but every thrust back inside was hard and demanding. He brought his arms up to grasp my shoulders from the front, holding me in place, and my first orgasm came timid and small, but a second one followed almost immediately after until every slow push of his cock sent a climax rushing through me, making a puddle form on the carpet underneath us. I'd lost count of how many times I came after the fifth one, but I wasn't ready to stop.

Arthur picked up his pace in Knight's ass, and he started jacking Knight's cock off in time with his thrusts. I kept coming, over and over, squirting and shaking, and it all rose until I felt like all the orgasms were leading to a bigger one, one that would be too much for me. I whimpered and Knight turned his head to me, so lost in passion his eyes were hazed over. I knew that look. Everything became too much, but I wouldn't beg for it to stop. I wanted everything.

"Come for her, Knight," Arthur ordered, and his hand on Knight's cock started pulling ropes of come out of the tip as he climaxed hard, screaming out Arthur's name.

Though I'd been having a constant orgasm for several minutes, I hit the plateau I'd felt rising and I was coming so hard, I felt like my spirit would leave my body, barely noticing Balthazar was biting into my shoulder as he shot his load inside me. He held me upright because my legs were useless at the moment and carried us both to the bed where we collapsed next to my spent lovers.

***

SOMEONE'S HAND on my leg stirred me awake, I hadn't even realized I'd fallen asleep. Arthur was near my face, Knight was behind me, and Balthazar was lounging beneath our feet. Sleepily, I leaned into Arthur and kissed his neck, running my fangs along his skin. I was definitely not in the mood for more sex, but I was always ready for kissing. He took my chin and guided me to his mouth, claiming my bruised lips as his, tugging me forward until I yelped because Knight's body was on top of my hair. When I reached back to free my curls, Arthur's phone went off somewhere in the room amongst our piles of clothes. He got up, retrieved it, and got back into bed before I could miss his warmth.

"Hello?" he said into the phone. His hand was lightly tracing up my leg, massaging my hipbone, when he froze stone cold. "What do you mean the castle is..." He was up in a fluid motion and off to his clothes, pulling his pants on while keeping the phone to his ear. The noise woke Knight up and he kissed my back before noticing Arthur's movements across the room. The vampire slid his phone into his pocket and zipped up the front of his pants. "Get dressed. All of you. We have to go."

I'd never seen him that serious before, it moved me off the bed and back to my clothes as Knight and Balthazar did the same. Dressed first, I approached Arthur who was madly texting on his phone and he jumped when I touched his arm. "Arthur, what's wrong?"

He didn't answer, he just leaned in and gave me a gentle kiss on the forehead before walking to the door and opening it with straight, deliberate movements. "Let's go."

We followed him out and down the stairs, Knight reaching to me to take my hand, and we stopped when Sara appeared from the sitting room, holding a large ice chest that looked heavy. Arthur took it and gave her a cautious once over.

"Did you know?" he asked, almost accusingly, and I wanted to smack the piss out of him until he told me what was wrong.

Sara seemed to know because she was matching his serious face and shuffled her slippers on the floor. "No. I only knew you'd be in danger if you stayed."

"Arthur, goddamnit, tell us what's happened," Knight shouted to him, his hand squeezing mine so tightly I winced.

My vampire lover turned and faced us, meeting only my eyes when he finally spoke. "There was a bombing at the castle. The Council is dead."

10

BACK IN CHARGE

*T*he car was silent on our way back. Arthur insisted on driving, leaving me in the backseat cuddled against Knight. I'd twisted in my seatbelt so my back was up against his chest, and he was tracing circles on my arm, kissing my head every few seconds. The Council meant nothing to him, but he knew Arthur and I were on edge, and he was desperate to be there for us.

"So, you and Arthur, hmm?" I said with a smile.

Arthur grunted at me from the driver's seat. "If you even *think* about teasing us, you have another thing coming, missy. You're the one that said we used to fuck, you're not allowed to be surprised."

"I didn't say you used to fuck. I said you were lovers. Mated lovers. Like, you bit him, and he bit you. I watched. Touched myself. Had a good time." They groaned and I giggled. "Just kidding. The children were there too. It was like a wedding ceremony."

"What about our wedding?" Knight asked in my ear, my responding arousal making the other men react.

"Knight, cool it. We have bigger things to worry about right now."

"Killjoy," I complained, snuggling closer to Knight, but Arthur was right. As much as I wanted to get them all naked again, it wasn't the time for that, and remembering what we were about to find sobered me enough that we all went silent again until hours later, Arthur pulled up to the castle.

Knight squeezed my shoulder as he looked out the window and I got up to see what he was looking at. The castle was badly damaged, flashing me back to the turned army attack when their missiles came at our home until nothing was left. This was very similar, but the structure was still there, barring a giant chunk of the top three floors that were blown out on the left side. Vampires were here and there amongst the rubble and I could see Olivier directing them where to go with their belongings.

I was the first out, rushing over to her and side-stepping large chunks of the building. Cameron was nearby with Renard, both safe, and I rushed up to them. With my hands holding Cameron's face, I looked him up and down just to be sure he was okay before giving him a chaste kiss on the lips and holding him close to me. My arms shook with the thought of him dying again.

"Lucky we weren't here," he soothed, putting his arms

around me. "It's okay, I'm okay." I was already sobbing, there was no holding it back. I'd never feel at ease with him now, I'd always be terrified of losing him a second time.

Arthur reached and gently took one of my wrists, and I took the hint, falling into his embrace instead, shaking against him as I tried to control myself. He rubbed my back and held me close with one arm while the other was all business. "They're all dead?"

Olivier answered. "We counted eleven bodies. There's no way the twelfth survived that close to the blast. He must've been blown out the window and crushed under one of the building pieces. We're searching for him."

Something didn't feel right. I couldn't say what it was but my senses were stirring and telling me there was something more. Arthur noticed my posture shift and he looked down at me. "What is it?"

I turned my head towards the castle and studied it, as if it would bring me some clarity, but it only made me more confused. "I don't know. I'm feeling something. Olivier, is it safe to walk up there?" She nodded, but before she could warn me against it, I was out of Arthur's shadow and approaching the open front doors.

"Lisbeth," Arthur protested, coming up behind me as I got to the foyer. He grasped my wrist again to stop me. "Lisbeth, no. Leave it alone. Let Olivier and myself investigate this."

Unwilling to fall to the sidelines now that my people had no leaders, I wrenched away from him and he almost looked hurt. "Where are the turned?"

Olivier opened and closed her mouth, not sure how to tell me the answer, and that was answer enough. "They're gone. They disappeared in the wreckage, we don't know what happened."

Facing the group in front of me, I met Arthur's eyes, the one who would understand this the most. "This wasn't just a bomb. This was Alistair. I'd bet everything on it. I'm going up, I need to see if the survivor left anything behind." I turned and started going up the stairs with my lovers and friends behind me. We made it to the right floor and approached the wreckage. "Renard, keep Cameron away."

"Olivier told me what happened to you," Cameron said pushing away from Renard's grip on him. "I died in your timeline, didn't I? That's why you're treating me like I'm made of glass."

Whirling on him, I felt flushed with anger fueled by my sadness, anger that he wasn't letting me protect him. "A human burned you and Knight's sister alive to make me submissive, so forgive me if I'm trying to keep you safe because I don't want to see you die again." Instantly regretting my harsh words, I felt like a fool, but I'd silenced his protests for the moment, and he stayed in the hallway while everyone who wasn't breakable walked further where the floor was more unstable.

"I like new Lisbeth," Olivier noted with approval. "She fights like a Hunter, she mouths off like a sailor. You guys better watch out, I might steal her from you."

"Not a chance," Arthur deflected with confidence.

The floor bowed beneath me, but I kept walking carefully until we reached the room where the bomb went off. Once several floors below the roof, it was now completely open to the sunlight, and ash danced around the air, landing on the bodies that lay covered with black sheets. I could smell where Castilla lay, half over a chair, and Othello by the door in a heap. My feet left prints on the dirty floor in my path to the center of the room.

"Marie is gone too. She was outside the door," Olivier told us, gesturing to her covered body that lay in the hallway, one I'd assumed was a bodyguard. My heart fell, remembering the way she'd made my mother happy. That would never happen now. "The blast came from here." Olivier walked up beside me, pointing to a spot near Castilla where the spray of black soot covering the room originated. I noticed the way my friend's body lay and wondered if she had been on the floor for a reason.

I stumbled slightly trying to get near her as the floor creaked dangerously, but I made it to her and lifted the blanket on top of her, trying not to see the way the bomb had all but destroyed one side of her body.

When the floor wobbled again, Knight tried to come protect me, but Arthur held him back. "Lisbeth, stop. What are you doing?"

I waved my hand back at Knight's fussing and turned to the side of Castilla's body that was intact. "She was right handed. If she took—" I grunted and reached underneath her for her hand. "If she took something from the bomb, it'll be... yes. Here." In her palm was a piece of paper and I retrieved it just as the charred half of her body disintegrated before my eyes. "Ahh, fuck. My mouth was open." Gagging, I stood up and brushed myself off, then I held the note out and returned to the safe part of the room. The floor buckled when I reached my mates and both Knight and Arthur grasped my arms to keep me upright as I stumbled forward.

We left for the hallway and I tried not to look at Marie's still form on the floor, focusing on opening the note, and my stomach plummeted to the ground when I saw what was written on it. I held it out, knowing no one would under-stand its significance like I would.

"This is Alistair's handwriting."

Arthur motioned for me to hand it over, and he squinted at the odd words on it. "What language is that?"

"No idea. I can't read psychopath. He probably made it up to keep people from reading his stuff. But it's a calling card. He was behind this. He knows we're after him and he's mobilizing far earlier than before. If we don't get a handle on him, he'll do much worse than this."

Arthur handed me the note back, his mouth in a grim twist. "There's another thing."

I folded the note up and stared back at him, knowing exactly where he was going with that. "Someone betrayed us. Someone was working with him, even in my time, and I didn't know it back then."

"We should find where the other vampires went," Knight offered, but I shook my head.

"No, Alistair won't be with them. He wasn't before, he won't be now. We have to…" I stopped and looked meekly at Arthur because he was going to hate this. "…find my mom."

"No way in hell," he declared, crossing his arms over his chest.

"I highly suggest not," Balthazar added, making Knight all the more curious who we were discussing.

"Care to clue us in about this mystery woman?" Olivier queried, looking from Arthur to me.

"My mom is Anastasia Bathory."

Her eyes grew wide in shock. "*Shit.*"

"Who dat?" Knight whispered in the stunned silence.

"She's a psychopath that almost destroyed vampires and let her mother die for her senseless crimes," Balthazar explained calmly, earning a scowl from me.

I held a warning finger up to him. "Watch it, sexy. I told you not to talk about my mom like that."

He winked and puckered his lips. "Make me."

Down, boy.

A plan forming in my head, I walked through the group and back down the stairs, all the way to Othello's old office that was my office now. Again. Whatever.

Coming up to the desk, I pushed papers out of the way on the wooden surface, revealing one of the squares I'd found before. Seeing everyone coming in behind me, I hurriedly swiped the Thinker statue from the fireplace mantle and put it in its place before rushing to my chair to grab the key.

"*Nice,*" Knight approved, whistling low. I pushed the key

into the hidden panel slot on the wall and it unlocked the hidden door beside the fireplace.

"How long has this been here," Arthur asked to my retreating back because I'd already gone inside the door into the dark study where Othello kept his book collection. Magically, the one I wanted was sitting on the lamp table like last time, and I grabbed it before coming back into my office and shutting the hidden door behind me.

Bringing it to the desk, I ripped the cloth binding off while everyone jumped forward to stop me, but I ignored them and tossed it aside, pulling the paper up that was stuck to the spine. I unfolded it to reveal the cloth that had my father's blood on it.

"Here, babe, smell this." I tossed it to Knight and stuffed the book into my back pocket. "It's going to kill you for a minute, but you'll be okay."

He eyed me like I'd gone insane. "What the fuck?" Saying that reminded me of the vision Sara had about him dying, but this was different. I still came up to stand in front of him though, just in case I was wrong. "What is this?"

"We have to make sure my dad is where I found him last time, and this is his blood. Sniff it up, we have to go." His face said I'd catch an earful about this later, but he put the cloth to his nose and sneezed all over it, dropping the cloth into my waiting hand as his eyes widened, his pupils dilated, and he started gasping for air. I was ready to catch him when his legs gave out and his lungs stopped moving. He was so much bigger than me but I was strong enough to keep him upright.

Arthur was instantly on both of us, looking as worried as I would've been if I hadn't done this before. "He's suffocating, Lisbeth, let me help him," he said, trying to remove the werewolf from my arms.

"Arthur, he's okay, I promise," I told him, adjusting Knight's towering body on me. "I know what I'm doing. I wouldn't do this if it hurt him, you know I wouldn't."

Knight's body came back to life with a loud gasp and his lungs started working again. "Fuck, that was trippy." He coughed several times and righted himself, standing on his own again. "Ahh, weird. I can see where your dad is. He's... eating Chinese food in a catacomb."

Typical dad.

With my answer found, we were free to pack our stuff up and travel to Paris. Everyone left to pack, but Cameron stayed behind in my office, no doubt to yell at me for being such a bitch.

"I'm sorry I yelled at you," I told him, trying to focus on the carpet in case he was mad at me.

His feet came up in front of mine and he leaned in to kiss my forehead. "I *love you*, Lisbeth. We're family. I can't even imagine what it was like for you to lose me like that. You can yell at me all damn day if you want to. I promise I'll stay safe while you're off saving the world, deal?" He held out a fist for me to bump, and we shared a smile before I leaned in, kissed him on the cheek, and held him so close to me, my arms ached. That's how we stayed until my three men returned with our bags, and we left the castle for the airport.

One of our private planes was waiting for us, and as we were the only passengers, we were free to pick any spot we wanted around the small cabin that seated about twenty people. Of course we chose to sit together, and we were close enough that I was able to rest my feet on the spot between Arthur's knees during takeoff.

The cheery voice announced we were free to move about the cabin, and Arthur undid his seatbelt, staring me down like I was a juicy rabbit he wanted to chase.

"Come here," he ordered firmly, making chills race over my skin.

I stood and defiantly reached under my dress, pulling my underwear off and flinging it at his head. "You're so fucking bossy." As he watched me, I turned to Knight sitting beside me and leaned over him, feeling the cold air on my exposed ass, and unzipped Knight's pants until his cock was free for me to sit on.

Arthur came up behind me, flipped me in his arms, and claimed my lips roughly as he backed me up to Knight's lap. Both of their hands on my ass guided me so Knight could slip his hard length inside my pussy. I kept Arthur's mouth on mine no matter how much he tried to pull away, until he tweaked my nipple through my dress, making me release his lips with a gasp. He deftly pulled my dress off me and tossed it into my seat, and the cold cabin air turned my nipples hard instantly.

Then Arthur knelt in front of my naked body, pulling my thighs apart so he could clearly see Knight's cock inside me.

He inhaled deeply, the ice behind his eyes melting at the sight of our joined bodies, and he leaned in to take one long lick from the underside of Knight's cock to the top of my slit. Knight moaned and bit into my shoulder from the sensation of Arthur's tongue on him, and I was doing the same. My hips jerked as Arthur sucked my clitoris into his mouth a few times before letting it go, blowing on it, and licking all around it to tease me.

Balthazar had been very silent up to now, content just to watch us, but when he saw me looking at him he opened his slacks and pulled his hard dick out, stroking it slowly up and down for me. His eyes took on a devilish hue when I felt something entering my ass, even though it was completely untouched. He was making me feel it, his drool worthy cock inside me, the very one I was looking at. My eyes rolled back and I groaned, loving the feeling of Knight in my pussy, Balthazar in my ass, and Arthur lapping at my clit. When my eyes opened again, I watched Balthazar's hand moving up and down his cock and the responding feeling in my ass mimicked his movements.

Knight had been still as Arthur continued licking both of us with his skilled tongue but with me squirming around, he was having a hard time waiting. Arthur pat on the werewolf's leg, not taking his mouth from me for one second, and Knight moved us forward just enough where he could start thrusting into me. He used one arm to secure my stomach, the other gripped my throat gently so I couldn't move away.

To punish Balthazar for teasing me, I dipped into his

head and made him feel every sensation rolling over my body. His nostrils flared and his hand rubbed his cock faster, making the one in my ass speed up. Arthur was careful to not lick my clit directly too much, but he had no idea what Balthazar was doing, and I was rising higher with every movement of his hand, despite Arthur's effort to keep me on the edge as long as possible. My walls pulsed hard around Knight, sucking him inside me, signaling I was very close.

"Fuck, Balthazar, I have no idea what you're doing, but keep it up, she's tightening around me, god damn it, I can't..." He bit my shoulder, drawing blood as he started coming inside me, thrusting up hard until he slowed down and fell back onto his chair, drained for the moment.

Arthur gave me one last lick, picked me up smoothly, and deposited me in Balthazar's lap now. My bare breasts rubbed against the soft cotton of his shirt and I licked a trail up his neck. A firm hand on my hair pulled me away, holding me upright on Balthazar's legs, making sure I didn't move as the Incubus slammed his full length into me. It only took a few thrusts before he started shooting ropes of come inside me, gripping my hips so hard it almost hurt.

Then it was the icy warrior's turn. He used my hair to pull me off of Balthazar's lap and brought me over to face his chair, putting my hands on either side of the headrest so he could run a hand down my bare ass, cracking one cheek and then the other. He slid inside my wet heat easily, positioning my feet far apart, making me unable to stay up without my hands on the top of his chair.

He brought his hand back to my hair and tugged it so my head was suspended in the air, my back arched, my breasts open for anyone to see. What would happen if someone walked in and saw Arthur fucking me from behind? They'd see my breasts bouncing with each push of his cock, they'd see my flushed skin and hear me moaning for more. I couldn't decide if that would turn me on more or if I'd be too embarrassed with a stranger's eyes on me.

Wet started streaming from me even though I was still climbing to a much needed climax. My body plateaued in pleasure and I was so close, almost there. A guttural moan came from my throat.

"P... Please," I pleaded almost too softly to hear. If Balthazar had been holding me back, he let me go, careening into bliss with my toes curling and my hands ripping into the fabric of the chair. Arthur kept me in place through my trembling and trying to grab anything so I wouldn't feel so exposed, but he wanted me to feel it. He wanted me to feel at his mercy as I came for him, and god, it was so hot. As I was catching my breath and coming down, he sped up his thrusts and slammed into my ass, coming hard for me.

It was at that moment I felt the icy hot burning in my belly, so powerful I was surprised at the intensity of it.

I cried out, in real pain this time, and Arthur released my hair, moving us to cradle me against him. Knight and Balthazar were already up on their feet to make sure I was okay, and they saw me clutching my stomach.

"I'm fine," I assured them, trying to straighten as the pain passed. "The potion just worked."

"You're pregnant?" Knight asked, and he smiled a smile that grew on all of our faces.

"I think so, yeah," I answered, just before they all swept me into a hug, covering me from all sides with their loving warmth. Arthur retrieved my dress, pocketing my underwear until I made him give it back, and I sat in Knight's lap once we were all decent again.

Knowing the potion had worked made me all the more terrified I was going to lose him again, for good this time. He could sense my worry, and he stroked my hair like he did in my time, pressing his face into mine so he could kiss at my skin without moving.

I fell asleep in his arms, like I wanted to do every day for the rest of my life.

11

BLOW, THOU WINTER WIND

*W*e landed in Paris many hours later and navigated towards the catacombs. Knight showed the same trepidation for them he had last time, and while I reached for his hand, Arthur held his back for the other without thinking about it.

They were so cute.

Balthazar had my other hand, and our little train entered the eerie tunnels with me navigating, Arthur leading the way, and Knight briefly confirming Lucas was in fact still in here. Navigating deep into the underground tunnels, we easily reached the beginnings of his den where it started to stink of old blood.

"*Grossss,*" Knight complained, unable to hold his nose with his lovers holding both of his hands. "It smells like rotten pennies in here."

"Good old dad," I remarked dryly, also not enjoying the smell.

Before it could reach a high enough potency in my nose to make me sick, we'd reached the right room and entered Lucas' lair where he sat doing Sudoku and munching on sunflower seeds. The fireplace was roaring with a warm fire, lighting the dark room up in orange flickers.

"Come in, come in," Lucas beckoned, not looking up from his book. "Could hear you complaining of the stench for five straight minutes. Honestly, don't you know it's rude to comment on someone's home like that?"

As he grouched at us, I let go of my lovers' hands and approached Lucas slowly until he glanced up at me, annoyed I was interrupting his puzzle. "Dad," I said to him, holding my hand out, trying to smile even though my body was shaking. I wasn't afraid of him, I was just so happy to see my father.

He looked at my hand like it was a grenade sent to murder him in his sleep. "You're mistaken, I don't have children." His deflection was ruined when he noticed who was behind me. "Ahh. Balthazar."

The blue eyed Incubus nodded in greeting of his old friend. Well. I say friend. "Lucas."

My father looked me over, really noticing me for the first time, taking in my dark curls and my purple irises, exactly like my mother's. He had bright, blonde hair with golden eyes, completely the opposite of me. "Never mind. Hello, Erzsébet."

"Lisbeth," I corrected, then waved my hand in dismissal. "It doesn't matter. Is mother in Čachtice with Clara?"

He sputtered, trying to recover from me knowing everything that I wasn't allowed to know. "Is who with the what? What are you chattering about, Lisbeth?"

"I don't have time for this. Arthur pick him up."

My icy warrior obliged, throwing my dad over his shoulder like he weighed nothing, then following behind me as I walked out of the doorway and back into the filthy tunnel.

"Noooo!" Lucas howled, bouncing with Arthur's every step. "I'll have your heads for this! This is no way to treat your father!" He beat his fists against Arthur's back.

"I see where you get your crazy side from," Arthur grunted under the pounding he was receiving.

"Eat me," I tossed over my shoulder.

IT WAS an hour before we were out and Lucas had finally calmed down, but Arthur didn't let him go until we were inside the airplane. Lucas chose a seat far away from us, pouting that I wouldn't listen to him about his constant trying to tell me he had no idea who Anastasia was.

We sat back in our original seats and I lifted up to check on Lucas before settling back in and leaning into my headrest. "God, this plane ride is not going to be as fun as the first one— *shit!*" As I was talking, my body shot off into a climax that almost made me fall out of my seat. "What the *fuck*, Balthazar!" He was the only one who could make me do that, so it was easy for me to stand up and smack my hand at him, but he only made me come again and my legs gave out, tossing me into Arthur's lap who was smirking like an *ass*. "I am going to get you both for— fuuuck..." I was coming again, harder this time until my body was shaking all over and I felt drained for the second time that day.

"Okay, ease up, guys," Knight said, rescuing me from Arthur's teasing arms. He nestled me against him with my legs across his lap. "Not that it's *not* hot to see you orgasm like that." I groaned and turned my head against his collarbone so I could catch my breath.

"Going to get you all back for that," I vowed weakly. "Damn it, I never had enough energy with just two of you, I'm going to need a week to recharge now with Balthazar in the mix."

"I'll be nice, my love," he promised, and I moaned again in thanks.

"I love you," I whispered, just so he knew I wasn't mad. "I love all three of you. Especially you," I finished, kissing Knight's hot neck.

"Stop touching my daughter!" Lucas roared, peeking over at us from his seat.

"Can't stop, won't stop," Knight retorted, making sure my dad saw him running a hand down my leg, and Lucas squeaked in indignant response. Marching down to sit in one of the seats beside us, he made a show of keeping an eye on everyone's hands during the plane ride, and my mates continued touching me randomly to piss him off.

Our plane touched down a few hours later and we got a rental car to drive us the extra hour to where my mother was. Lucas never stopped muttering to himself, squished between Arthur and Knight in the backseat as I drove.

We arrived in the fateful city my grandmother lived in all those centuries ago. Beside me, Balthazar stiffened as it all came into view, and he probably would've disappeared into thin air if he hadn't fallen in love with me. Despite our new feelings, I knew this couldn't be easy for him, and I took one hand off the steering wheel to put on top of his, entwining our fingers until he relaxed enough that I knew he would be okay.

When I pulled up to the small cottage squished between two large houses, Lucas' mutterings got louder until I had to twist back and tell him to be quiet. "Dad," I said when that didn't work. "Remember what we said? In my time you and Clara were married. She'll forgive you. Please calm down." He nodded, but his body remained frigid and taunt.

We'd told him everything on the plane ride over since he wouldn't stop bothering us. He took it all in stride and believed it without much effort, especially liking the part about Clara forgiving him. Clara meant everything to him, if he didn't have her love in his life, he had nothing. I knew the feeling well. My dad and I were a perfect pair.

"Haul out, fam."

"I don't respond to the word, *'fam'*," Arthur mentioned in complaint.

"Move it, sexy ass," I ordered with a shake of my finger at him.

Everyone was out and onto the sidewalk in record speed, and we stood in front of the door that led to both of my moms. My normal mom, and my step-mom/aunt. My feet were frozen to the ground even though I was more than excited to have my moms so close to me. I knew Anastasia was still lost inside her mind, and it would be up to me to wake her up. It had been hard the first time, it would be equally hard the second time.

Behind me, Knight slid his hands around my stomach, resting his chin on my head like he used to in my time, and my other two lovers put their hands on my arms to steady me. They were all here with me. I could do this.

I stepped up to the door and rapped on the wood, putting my hand firmly at my side when it started shaking. It took a few moments, but the door opened and Clara was there, looking beautiful with her golden hair and her soft, gentle face. I launched myself into her perfect arms and I cried onto her blue dress. Naturally, she was confused as to why a stranger was hugging her and getting her dress wet with tears, but I felt her body stiffen as she saw the group behind me.

"Lucas? Balthazar?" Her breath caught and her small hands came up to my sides as she realized who I was. "Elisabeth?" I sobbed as an answer. "Oh my god, it's you. You've come back to us." She tapped my side, signaling for me to let her go even though I didn't want to. We'd travelled the few footsteps into the house so she gestured for the men to follow us, flushing slightly when Lucas passed her and she could shut the door behind him.

My attention had been torn away because Anastasia was sitting quietly by the fire, as still as a statue since we came in. I left everyone in the doorway and approached her, sitting beside her and checking her blank face. She was still lost.

My family chattered behind me and I tuned them out as I tried to think of what to say to wake her up this time. Before, she'd woken up to the scent of Knight's blood, but she almost attacked him and she was crazy powerful. I wouldn't risk him being hurt.

"Who told her?"

"There's something you should know."

I picked up Anastasia's hand and felt her rough skin, scratched and marred from her life, just like she was. Clara had clearly just cleaned her up and dressed her in a simple, black shirt with pants so her gothic dress could be cleaned, the one she wore when she wandered around town like a creepy ghost.

"...the witches sent her back..."

"...we've come to try and stop what happened..."

I started humming a tune my mother had sung to Gwen when she was a baby, standing in my daughter's room and slowly rocking back and forth on her hips to comfort Gwen's baby tears. I wanted my mother back just as much as I wanted my baby in my arms.

The rest of the room went silent after they'd explained everything to Clara, so I felt safe to sing the song aloud, clutching Anastasia's hand through every word with my eyes closed, remembering her with my baby and hoping that image would return.

Blow, blow, thou winter wind,
Thou art not so unkind
As man's ingratitude;
Thy tooth is not so keen,
Because thou art not seen,
Although thy breath be rude.
Heigh-ho! sing, heigh-ho! unto the green holly:
Most friendship is feigning, most loving mere folly:
Then, heigh-ho, the holly!
This life is most jolly.

Freeze, freeze, thou bitter sky,
That dost not bite so nigh
As benefits forgot:
Though thou the waters warp,
Thy sting is not so sharp
As friend remembered not.
Heigh-ho! sing, heigh-ho! unto the green holly:

Most friendship is feigning, most loving mere folly:
Then, heigh-ho, the holly!
This life is most jolly.

Halfway through the song, I heard someone humming along with me until they joined in at the chorus and we harmonized beautifully. I thought it was Clara, until I heard her join in as well, matching the tune and harmonizing a third part, trailing the song off with us in unison.

I opened my eyes to see Anastasia, her purple eyes clear and wide open, smiling at me, knowing instantly who I was. "My baby," she whispered, holding her hand out for me, and I fell into her, clutching her so close my arms ached. All the sadness I'd felt over losing my babies poured out of me in my mother's embrace, because if anyone could make this better, it was her. We'd had a rocky start in my time, spent so many years apart, but in the end she was there for me, just like I'd always wanted my mother to be. She'd even raised my son for me when I couldn't get to him.

I'd never realized how much I loved her.

She didn't understand my pain, but she didn't need to. We'd tell her my story and I'd still feel like staying in her arms until everything was okay again, like a small child who wakes up during the night, scared of the thunder outside. And that's just what happened. Everyone came near the fire and the men that loved me explained everything to her, and through it all, my mother never wavered in her embrace of me, her gentle stroking of my long hair, even when they told her what I'd said about our first meeting. She clutched me tightly when they spoke of my children and losing them to come here.

When the story was finished, she held me closer and kissed my head. "My Erzsébet, you've been through so much. I'm glad your new journey still led you to me. Will someone hand me the journal you spoke of?" Knight got up from where he was sitting nearby and went outside, returning with the book from the car that he handed to Anastasia who lifted one of her hands off of me to retrieve it.

"Your lovers are handsome," she noted appreciatively, opening the journal with one hand. "The werewolf reminds me of my Nicolas." Her eyes flicked over the words and she expertly turned the pages with her thumb, understanding the odd language that was written there. "It seems this Alistair was quite the mastermind. He gave me the slip for a very long time. Cat and mouse, fish and bait."

She turned more pages and stopped, straightening slightly from what she was reading. "I mention your son, Jason." I jumped up and bent over the words, but I couldn't read any of it. "I found him destitute and alone, and he clung to me like a boy who lost his mother." Fresh tears built in my eyes and she put a comforting hand on my arm, still reading. "I raised him for my daughter, as I wished I could have raised her when she was as small as he. He's strong, like her. Loving. Kind. I'm proud to have a grandson as grand as him." She smiled, flipped the page and squeezed my arm, finished with the part about Jason. "I cannot wait to meet this boy, my love," she said warmly, then she went back to reading. "I'll need some time to look over all of this," Anastasia declared after several minutes. "I know time is pressing, but this is very complex. If there's an answer on where to find him, it will take some work to dig it out."

"In the meantime, we should get back to the castle," Arthur said somewhere above me. "We're defenseless with it damaged and it won't be fixed overnight."

I looked up at Knight and it gave me an idea, prompting me to my feet. "We'll bring everyone back with us so you're nearby when you find the answer."

"Lisbeth, your mother is a criminal," Arthur pointed out.

Anastasia scoffed under her breath. "I'm cooling on that one."

"Then I pardon her. You're pardoned. And you're pardoned too, dad."

He pumped his fist in triumph. "Yess! That's my girl!"

I expected Arthur to protest, but he knew how the chain of command worked. With Othello gone, I took his place, and what I said was law. There was no way around it. He had to obey me, and not just because there was pussy on the line.

"Also," I started, checking his face first. "I'm going to negotiate a truce with the Lycans."

He breathed deeply and his jaw worked a few times before he met Knight's eyes and he softened up. "I'd like that too." They shared a significant look that made me warm all over, because it was clear to anyone with eyes that they were falling in love with each other again.

"Awwwww," I cooed, putting my fists to my mouth in a cute gesture, batting my eyelashes at Arthur.

"Zip it," he warned, but I was already approaching him, pulling on the back of his neck so I could reach his lips, and we kissed tenderly until Lucas saw and made that squeaking noise again.

"Hands off daughter! Off!"

"Lucas, grow up," Anastasia bossed from the floor.

"If she didn't say it, I was going to."

Anastasia looked up when the Incubus spoke, and she stood to face him, her face looking deathly still again. "Balthazar," she said with a nod to him. The tension between them was as thick as a cow's ass.

"Awkward," Knight whispered through his teeth.

Moving first, Balthazar closed the distance between them, and he diplomatically held his hand out to my mother, surprising everyone, least-wise me, considering even in my time they still weren't friends.

"What happened with the Countess was the direct result of her own choices. She made the choice to stray from me and that resulted in you and your sister. I hated you for that, but it wasn't your fault. After what happened to her, I used to believe you were selfish for letting her take the fall for you, but I have since learned that there is no shame in protecting the people you love. I begged her in the end for you to turn her, and she refused, again making her own choices that had nothing to do with you. And now, I'm afraid I've fallen in love with your daughter, so if you wish for me to be gone because the sight of me offends you, that is something I cannot do."

Anastasia blinked a few times, looking down at his offered hand, and choosing her words carefully, the way I'd always seen her react to things. "You stayed with my mother in that tower until she died, and I will always be grateful for that. You looked after my daughter when I could not, and now you stand by her side to protect her like you protected the Countess when I failed to do so. There are not many souls I would trust with my child, but I suppose you've proven yourself worthy of it."

The room went eerily still and Clara broke it with a gentle sob. "Oh Ana, that was lovely."

Balthazar quirked his mouth at her. "Mine was nice too."

And then Anastasia took his hand and they shook, finally allies.

WE HAD to stay the night, mostly because Clara insisted, but also the flight crew of our private plane needed rest. We women went to the kitchen area to make dinner, even though I insisted that was super sexist and the men could cook too, but Clara threatened me with a rolling pin until I agreed to help.

The men were around the fire, sipping some wine Clara had been saving for a special occasion. As I helped roll out dough, an apron tied around me and my hair back in a ponytail, whenever I checked on the men, one of mine was always looking at me, and heat was rising inside me that had nothing to do with the oven being on.

I could tell something was up when even Knight had a gleam in his eyes, and their casual façade didn't fool me. Anastasia and Clara moved away to do something at the sink and as soon as their backs were turned, I flew forward and banged my head on the counter as I started climaxing under Balthazar's powers.

Mother fuckers.

I grit my teeth at them with Clara and Anastasia fussing over me and checking my forehead. I took my apron off and knew exactly how I'd get my revenge. It was something I'd come up with in the future during one of my countless fucks with Knight and Arthur.

Leaning against the counter, I squared the three men with a look and motioned with my hand for them to bring it. Pushing my powers out, I knew when Balthazar sent the order for me to orgasm again, and I deflected it back to them, making all three instantly come in their pants and they tried to hide it with mock coughing.

When they'd recovered and gave me indignant looks in the brief moment my parents weren't looking, I held up my middle fingers for their approval.

"What are you four doing?" Anastasia reproached when she saw me flipping the bird.

I put my hands down and smiled innocently. "Nothing." She smelled my bullshit and handed me a handful of silverware with cloth napkins and pointed to the table. Ahh, good old mom. Putting me to work like I was a ten year old. Turning my backside to my men, I started setting the table, straightening everything three times before I was satisfied.

Knight approached once I was done, putting an arm around me and kissing my head. "I have to go."

Before I could ask, Clara almost dropped her pan of steaming hot potatoes. "But we haven't started dinner yet!"

Anastasia seemed to know what was up a second before I did. "Is it the full moon tonight? I still don't have my bearings yet."

Knight kissed me again and hovered over me, stroking my cheek. "I'll be back later." He tried to leave but I held onto him.

"No, I'm coming too." Checking Arthur's face, he nodded to me and I walked with Knight to the door, shutting it behind us so we were alone under the chilly, darkening sky.

"You went with me a lot?" he asked, holding my hand tightly.

"The only time Jason shifted was during this time of the month. He wanted to be there for you. Sometimes we went together. I just… the Knight in my time never ran alone. I don't want you to be alone."

He tried to smile, but he was afraid. "I might hurt you."

"No, you would never do that. You're not dangerous, I promise you."

His face lit up with a choked ironic laugh. "You said I throat punched you the first time you saw me shift."

"Yeah, well, that notwithstanding, the other times were fine." The mirth on my face only faded when he came closer and put his hands on my neck, holding me a breath's width above his lips. I waited for him to kiss me, but instead he leaned down, his lips against my neck, and he bit into my skin, marking me as his mate. Moaning from the pain, I held him to me until he let me go and resurfaced with droplets of my blood on his mouth that I reached up and kissed away.

"There," he pronounced, wiping my cheek from the tears that had fallen. "Now you're safe. I won't hurt you. Even if you believed I wouldn't, I won't risk your safety." He held out his hand for me and we walked down the street, making the long walk out of town where he would be safe to change into his primal form.

We made it up to the ruins of my grandmother's castle and I made sure we were alone when Knight removed his clothing and folded them into a pile by some benches that he could come back to when dawn arrived. The moon hadn't risen yet, but it would come very soon, and Knight was agitated waiting. He stood looking out over the land before us with acres of trees and flowers, and I came up behind him, putting my arms around his waist, surveying the land of my birth with him.

He let out a breath and put his hand on top of mine on his stomach. "I love you so much, Lisbeth." Turning in my arms, he slowly bent over me and kissed my lips like he was trying to memorize their shape. "I've been alone for so long, no one ever accepted me exactly as I was until you came. I know I disliked you at first, but you put my needs over yours at every second, and I fell so deeply in love with you, I never want to find my way out." He brushed at my tears and my chin trembled under his touch. "You said I was everything to you. You're my very existence now. And if my moments from here on out are measured, I want every breath to belong to you. Every heartbeat. Everything."

With me unable to form words for the tears streaming down my face, his hands found the sides of my dress and he pulled it up over my head, dropping it and my underwear on the stony path, and he guided me back until I was pressed against one of the stone walls. Our lips parted as he took measured breaths, trying to hold himself back, but I wasn't going to let him. Putting my hands on his shoulders, I jumped up and he was forced to grip my thighs to keep me in his arms.

Steadying me with one arm around my waist, he used the other to align himself with my entrance, and he pushed me into the wall, pushing inside me with the same movement. He made slow and gentle love to me in the shadows, kissing down my neck, biting my hard nipples, and staring into my eyes like I was the only woman in the world he had ever wanted.

I kissed him deeply, feeling the pleasure rising inside me, his thrusts raking against my walls and driving me insane with his unhurried pace. I connected our minds so he would feel exactly what it felt like being in his arms, having his cock inside me, and his lips pressed to mine. The added sensations coming from him turned the tide on my pleasure and it rose higher until I could feel Knight struggling to hold off his climax for me but unable to resist the powerful tingles coming from the base of his cock, and we went over the edge together, coming inside me and shuddering around him, so connected I hardly knew which body was mine.

He had to let me down because both our legs had turned to jelly, and we sat on one of the benches until our hearts went back to a normal rhythm. Well, mine did. Knight's sped off again when he saw the clouds part in the sky and his other girlfriend started appearing. I used his momentary stillness to get dressed again and stayed a safe distance away when his body started shifting. His nose grew to a snout, his skin sprouted long black hairs, and his feet malformed to an odd angle that only added to his towering height.

When he was fully turned, he howled at the moon in his bipedal wolf form and my spine shivered at the sight of him. He was as beautiful as always.

The wolf Knight turned to me and took a long whiff of my scent, walking up to me carefully and looking me over. He was in there, I knew he was, but he didn't have the control he'd had in my time. It would come eventually, he just needed practice.

Wolf Knight approved of me and leaned down to nuzzle my neck where his bite was. His fur was so soft under my hands, and I found that spot on his belly he liked for me to scratch because it made his leg pump up and down like a dog. He did so, his tail wagging behind him appreciatively in time with his leg. Before I could finish, he scooped me up with his paw and put me on his back. I had just enough time to put my arms around his neck before he took off running, away from the castle and into the trees we'd been looking at.

I'd warned him in his human form about the pack that lived nearby, but wolf Knight would know to stay away when he smelled their pee line that marked their territory. I trusted he would keep us safe as he darted through the trees, jumping over fallen logs and reaching up to swing on the tree branches like a monkey.

This was the Knight I remembered from our early days, the carefree one who was free to be a wolf and didn't have to focus on anything unless he was threatened. Somehow this seemed more his true form, even if his brain was temporarily turned off. The only thing that stopped me from never wanting to work with him on controlling his shifts was knowing how terrified he was after he woke up in the morning, not knowing what he'd been doing during the night.

Wolf Knight tirelessly ran through the forest, but I wasn't tireless, and I fell asleep on his back at some point. I woke up, sure I'd fallen off somewhere, but I was stretched out on one of the castle benches and the sun had already risen. Knight stood on the edge of the cliff overlooking the valley, fully clothed, and I got up to stand beside him.

"Sorry I wore you out," he joked with a smile.

Taking his elbow, I turned him until he faced me. "I won't let you die. You're not leaving me. Ever. We still have children to make, we have a life to live. I want sixty-seven years with you, and then sixty-seven more."

He leaned down to me, pressing our foreheads together in the morning sunlight, his arms coming up to grasp mine. "No matter what happens, I'm not leaving your side. You, Arthur, and Balthazar are my world." He gently kissed my forehead, holding me there until my hands stopped shaking, then he stepped back and led us down the path away from the castle.

The town was just waking up around us with roosters crowing and a herd of geese crossing the road from one pond to another. We sidestepped them and they squawked in complaint, flapping angrily at us until we ran down the rest of the street, turning right and seeing my parents' house still in the cool shadows.

Arthur sat on the front step, standing up when he saw us. I was almost worried something had happened while we were gone, but when his icy blue eyes were fixed on Knight, I realized he'd been worried about him.

Still with our hands clasped, Knight came right up to the vampire and they bent their heads close, resting their foreheads together and sliding a hand across their backs in a loving embrace. I almost felt like I was intruding on a private moment and I didn't break their contact until Knight tugged me between them and they kissed me before kissing each other over my head.

I never wanted moments like these to end. I wanted to be in their arms forever, except we were missing someone.

"Where's Balthazar?" I asked with my mouth against Knight's shirt.

Arthur grew rigid and his hand moved from Knight's hair to mine. "He's with your parents. They had a talk."

I stiffened too, and groaned. "Fuck, what now?" He didn't answer, he just led us both by our hands inside the house where my three parents sat with Balthazar at the kitchen table, and the looks on all of their faces filled me with dread.

"There's some plates in the fridge," Clara said quietly, her expression showing she didn't approve of whatever they were discussing, her eyes darting to Anastasia every few seconds with a frown.

I walked up to Balthazar, putting my hand on his shoulder while Knight and Arthur went to the kitchen and started heating up the leftovers waiting for us. "Out with it. What's got you four so upset?"

Anastasia folded her hands on the table in front of her and tapped her index finger on the faded wood. "You cannot have an Incubus as a lover." She interrupted my response before I could get out more than a surly, "*Oh come on!*" I glared at her, feeling exactly like I had the first time we met when she tried bossing me around without trusting me. "He is too virile, delicately speaking. You risk a pregnancy every time you're with him, and he understands that you can't just keep popping out babies for the rest of your life, especially if the Bicus find out he's making more children when they're banned from doing so."

"I can't even *begin* to believe what I'm hearing. I've said this to you before, but since you weren't there for it, let me say it again. *You can't tell me what to do.*" Her face turned stone cold but she didn't respond.

In the silence, Balthazar stood, the look on his face turning my stomach. "She's right, Lisbeth. I'm not willing to abandon you, I'm bound to you now. I've agreed to go back to the Bicus realm and ask my leaders if there is anything to be done about my virility, and I don't care what the cost is, I will pay it a million times over."

My body went into a cold sweat and tears rolled down my cheeks. "But time moves differently there. You might not come out again for years."

"And I might be there for an eon while only a second passes for you. It won't matter how much time passes, it won't change how I feel about you. And I swear..." He gripped my waist and bent so our lips were almost touching, his hands trembling where they touched me. "I swear when I return I will never leave your side again."

My lungs burned with unreleased sobs. "What if you miss the birth of our daughter?"

"I'll do everything I can to make sure I don't. And if I do, I expect you to show me every moment." He finally bent enough for me to kiss him, tenderly dancing our lips together, my salty tears mixing in with the taste of lilacs. Only it wasn't lilacs anymore. He smelled like the sweet scent of lavender in the sunshine.

He smelled like me.

Before I was ready, he lifted from my lips and held my

head to his chest. I felt my other men behind me, and Balt-hazar addressed them as he stroked my hair. "I don't know when I'll be back. Please take care of her while I'm gone. Arthur, if something happens... I leave her to you." He put me at arm's length and waited until Arthur and Knight had me anchored with their arms around me before he disappeared.

12

THE SEARCH BEGINS

*I*t was an odd sensation, missing someone who I'd never truly missed before. Throughout my long life, Balthazar had always flitted about, popping in a few times a year, going sometimes months between visits. I had grown to expect his absence, and it wasn't something I got upset about. That was all out the window now. Now I missed him like someone had torn my arm off.

I sat alone at the back of the plane, staring out the window with my legs curled under me, stroking at the Bathory crest necklace Clara had given me again. I'd lost it along the way in my time and I was glad to have it back, but it didn't fix my mood.

Anastasia approached me, standing in the aisle with her hand on the seat opposite me. "Can I join you?" I didn't answer so she took it as approval and came to sit across from me. "I know you're mad at me." I still didn't say anything, mostly because I knew I'd say something mean if I did. "While you were out with your lover, I was reading that journal you brought me. I wrote about what happened to your family when Balthazar was arrested. It left your young son on his own. Your family left you for five years to bring him back. You suffered because of that. If he doesn't do something, you will suffer again. They'll take him away for good and then you'll wish you'd tried to fix it sooner." She paused and sighed, drawing my eyes to her, and she had a thoughtful look on her face. "The way he looks at you. He never looked at my mother like that. You let him cherish you, protect you. Mother never allowed him to behave that way with her. Even in her last days she kept him at arm's length, never letting him truly possess her. I wonder what that was like for him, finally falling in love after thousands of years, only for her to never fully accept him in her heart."

A fresh wave of sadness overcame me and I reached out my hand for her to take, gripping her fingers tightly across our seats. "I know you're just trying to protect me. I would've done the same to protect my children too." I got up and sat on the armrest beside her, holding her close to my breast, mostly for my own strength, but also for hers because of what I was about to say.

"I need to tell you about someone. Her name was Marie."

AFTER A VERY LONG story that involved many tears and a pile of used tissues, I fell asleep in my mother's lap.

I dreamed about that birthday party again, the same dream I'd had on my wedding night where my four children were outside the farmhouse setting up for my birthday. I walked out of the house again, wearing a white cotton dress and flowers in my hair, seeing a grown Gwen turn from her work and coming up to me. She was so beautiful.

"Mother, we're about to start," she told me, tugging me forward to the decorated table.

Kitty was busy setting out saucers for the servings of cake, but she looked up when we were near the table. "Mother," she said with a nod and a smile.

Jason and Dreya appeared from behind some bushes and my son kissed my cheek. He was so warm and real. "Happy birthday, mother."

Dreya smiled lovingly at me, checking above my head for the color of my aura. "Happy birthday, mother," she echoed.

They were all four around me, so close I could, and did, reach out to touch them.

"Give her some room, kids," Knight's voice said from behind me. I turned to see him, and I knew deep inside that this was the Knight I knew now, not the one I'd spent a lifetime with. "You know how she feels about birthdays."

I didn't question what this was, I simply closed the distance between us and kissed my husband passionately on the lips, much to the chagrin of our children.

"Stop complaining," Knight chided to them, putting his

large hands around my waist. "Once your other dads get here, we're all going to make out, and you'll just have to deal with it."

Confused, I bent back to look up at his face. "Other..." The roar of an engine grew louder in my ear until it stopped at the end of the unpaved road. Two men got out, Arthur and Balthazar, both holding bouquets of flowers. "It didn't happen like this the first time," I said out loud.

Knight chuckled at me, kissing the top of my head. "It was always meant to be this way. You just didn't stay long enough last time to see."

Arthur reached me first and handed me his bundle of roses, kissing my cheek long enough until my body lit up like a lightboard. "Happy birthday, love."

Balthazar had enough lavender to fill the house, and he pushed Knight and Arthur aside to have my full attention as he swept me up in his arms, bent me backwards, and kissed me until my knees were weak. "I love you more than life itself, my pet. Happy birthday."

When I resurfaced, Arthur was kissing Knight so hard, I was surprised the kids weren't complaining again, but they'd busied themselves at the table, purposefully giving us our privacy for the moment. Balthazar left my arms and completed the embrace of the other two men, leaning his forehead against theirs, but before I could ask why he was touching them like that, a hand on my shoulder woke me up on the plane.

Knight was leaning over my sleeping form and my

mother stirred as I did. "We've landed." He helped me up and I rubbed my eyes, a smile on my face. "Good dream?"

Standing, I pressed my hands on his chest after Anastasia had gotten up and passed us, heading to the entrance of the plane. "It was one I've had before, in the other time. It was different though. Better. Not like it had changed, just gotten bigger. Also I'm pretty sure you woke me up before you hardcore made out with Balthazar."

Even though I was partially joking, Knight contemplated that with a distant smile. "He's a pretty hot dude, I could do worse."

"You have *never* said the words '*hot dude*' before."

He drew me closer, lightly pressing our lower halves together until I felt his excitement, hard and waiting. "Better get used to it. This is all your fault."

His head dipped until we kissed again and again. "I'm sooo..." I started, moving my hips in a circle against him. "...*guilty.*"

"I can't leave you two alone for five seconds." Arthur's heavy footsteps approached until he was right behind me. "We have to *go*. Remember that part? We can tear her clothes off later." He turned to lead us out so I jumped up on his back, putting my arms around his neck. "I can only imagine what our kids will be like," he said without pausing for one second down the plane aisle.

"They're *awesome*, because I'm awesome. And you're awesome. And Knight is awesome. And Balthazar is awesome. Therefore, our kids are awesome. It's science in play, Arthur."

"I will drop you off the plane."

I grumbled a moan and held him tighter when he started going down the plane steps. "Spoil sport." I pressed my lips to the back of his neck. "You know you love me." Grunting, he tried to put me down once we were on the ground, but I held on until he carried me all the way to the baggage claim where my parents were waiting. Lucas looked green at the sight of me touching a man, and Anastasia raised a judgmental eyebrow at me on my lover's back.

"Lisbeth, how old are you? Honestly."

"You mean in this timeline, or this one plus the other? Because if we're going by that logic, I'm older than all three of you now." I emphasized my point by playfully gnawing on Arthur's thick shoulder.

When my parents had all turned to grab their bags on the conveyer belt, I let out a sigh and rested my chin on Arthur's shirt. I'd let myself forget for a few moments about Balthazar being gone, Knight's impending demise, and the fact we still had to save the world, the entire reason I was brought here.

Sensing my mood shift, Arthur squeezed my legs where he was holding them up and turned his head enough so he could kiss me on the cheek. Knight had gone ahead to get our bags as well, leaving us by ourselves in the terminal.

"It's going to be just us soon, isn't it," I said mournfully.

Arthur sighed and adjusted me against him. "You're assuming the witch was right. I don't believe it. I won't. We can't have found each other again only to lose everything a second time. Look at us, Lisbeth. You brought two strangers back to you who had no reason to stay by your side. That has to mean something. I won't believe fate could be so unkind."

I rubbed my nose against his cheek and felt my wet tears on his skin. "You're always so eloquent when you're in love."

He kissed my cheek again, running his face along mine in a caress. "And even if I'm wrong, I'll love you enough for both of them. You can count on that."

The warmth in my heart was almost enough to erase the pain. I reached my hand up and stroked at his short blonde stubble. "I can always count on you." Having found our bags, Knight returned to us and he threaded his arms through Arthur's until his hands rested on my back, hugging both of us at once.

"Son-in-laws," Lucas piped up in a huff upon seeing our group snuggle. "You can hug later, let's go. I need more pocky."

Stepping down onto the floor, we walked hand in hand behind my parents to the parking lot where we'd left the Impala. It was a tight fit with an extra person, but with the women in the middle of each seat, the men were able to make do with the space left. Lucas was especially happy neither of my lovers could touch me since he'd claimed the front seat to be near Clara.

Thankfully, it was only a short drive from the airport, and it ended when the castle came into view, lit by the setting sun. It was still jarring to look at the damage, but I could see some extra supports underneath the floor where the bomb went off. Most of the building chunks on the lawn had been removed, the large gashes in the ground the only reminder they'd been there. We got out of the car and we approached the front steps where Olivier stood waiting for us.

She curtseyed to me, nodding respectfully. "Madam Lisbeth."

God, not that again.

"Just Lisbeth," I reminded her. "Any updates?"

She raised her head and started biting one of her brown lips, briefly flicking her eyes to Arthur. "I contacted the Lycans like you asked me to." That was news to me, drawing my attention to Arthur who had his gaze fixed straight ahead. "I'd just like to point out that everyone is pissed off about it, so whatever you were trying to accomplish isn't working."

"We're trying to accomplish peace," Arthur informed her, silencing her with his piercing stare.

"Yeah, this is why we don't date anymore," Olivier responded, pulling her middle finger out of her pocket for him.

Trying not to laugh, I pat his arm like he was an unruly puppy. "Down, boy."

"They haven't responded, but I'll let you know when they have," she continued, eyeing Arthur like she wanted to slug him. "Also everyone knows about her." She gestured with her chin to my mother, still with the attack face. "I think they're more pissed about that."

"Could you show my parents to a suite?" She nodded to me and was off, leading them inside. I faced my men and found Knight's face drawn to the darkening sky.

"I'll have to go soon," he said. "I'll be fine alone, I promise." Arthur and I came to him at the same time, and we held him together, kissing and hugging him before he stepped away. "See you in the morning." We watched him retreat off the lawn and down the street before he disappeared into the forest.

Knowing I'd be worried sick until he returned, I immediately went into planning mode. I wasn't going to get any rest, I might as well do something useful. Arthur left to check the castle guard and I went to my office where I found a rolled up map of the world in one of the cabinets. I recovered a rolling cork board from the smaller drawing-room, sticking the map to it with pushpins.

Anastasia had given me some translated notes from her journal and I used them to mark off places on the map where she knew Alistair wasn't hiding, and all the places that he'd used to trick her into thinking it was his lair when it had just been a trap. I'd been there for hours when Arthur came in and flicked on the office light.

I barely glanced at him, still trying to decipher a word my mother had written. "Come here. Is this an R or an N?" He approached the board and surveyed my work. I felt proud when he didn't look unimpressed. He didn't look impressed either, but I took my pluses where I could. I picked my marker up again to put another X on the board but he stopped me, taking the papers from my hands and setting them down on the chalk tray.

"It's time for bed, let's go."

I shook my head and tried to pick my things up again, squirming in his arms when he blocked me. "No, I can't sleep with Knight gone. Let me work."

"Oh, we're not going to sleep. I can assure you of that."

And like that, work mode went away like it never existed, and my body was alive like someone had stuck me with an electric wire. Arthur walked towards me, looking like a tiger chasing his prey and forcing me to step backwards until my ass hit the edge of my desk, but he kept moving, pushing my knees apart and standing between them.

"Did I ever fuck you in here?" he asked, his large hand coming up to grip one side of my neck. I shook my head, unable to speak with him staring at me like I was a meal he would devour in one swallow. "I bet you thought about it. Thought about me shoving you against this desk, fucking you from behind on it, maybe even tying you up so you can't escape." The way my pulse shot off like a rocket gave me away, that I might not have thought of those things before, but I definitely was now. He chuckled at me with a teasing grin. "I've only had you a few times, but you get so damn wet when you're helpless beneath me. You like being at my mercy. You're not like that with Knight or Balthazar. You want them to fuck you. You want me to take you." His other hand ran down my side until he slid it underneath me, grasping my ass cheek roughly. "Tell me I'm wrong." My voice was completely gone and he squeezed me again when I didn't answer.

"You're not," I said hoarsely, ending in a moan as he lifted me up by my neck until I was level with his mouth. I wanted to close the distance between us but he held me in place.

"Tell me what you want me to do to you," he commanded, every breath mingling with mine.

"I want you to fuck me exactly the way you think of doing every time I'm a smart ass. Like I'm only here to be fucked by your cock." The words burned every inch of my skin, and I knew he would give me all of that and more.

"*Shit,*" he swore, and crushed my lips with his, devouring me whole, his grip on my neck starting to hurt. He quickly turned me around, ran both of his hands down the globes of my ass and reached underneath my dress to tear my panties off me. He tossed the ruined scrap of cloth away and removed my dress next until I was naked, the cold office air making me tingle. "Down against the desk." I bent and pressed my bare front across it, my cheek warm on the cold wood.

He left me for a moment but I stayed where I was, knowing he would be cross if I moved. When he returned, he took my hands back behind me and secured them with bonds strong enough to hold a vampire, making me at his mercy as I'd wanted to be. He wasn't finished, however. He knelt behind me and started tying my ankles together, then my thighs. From my position on the desk, even with my legs bound my slit was exposed to him.

With my head to the side, he stood in front of me and I watched him unbutton his pants, dropping the zipper, and pulling his cock out. He stroked it up and down, swirling his thumb against the head, staring right into my eyes.

"When I first met Knight after you told me he'd been my lover, I pictured what it would be like to fuck him. What noises he would make, how tight his ass would be." Jesus, he was really going to just talk while I was lying here tied up. I was impossibly even more turned on from the neglect. "That didn't prepare me for the real thing, though. When I had him underneath me, he whimpered, waiting for me to put my cock inside him. He wanted it, and he'd never even touched another man before." Arthur's hand slowly stroked up his length, his hips thrusting forward slightly. "And when I pushed inside him, his cock jerked from the feeling of a man's dick rimming his ass. I don't think you noticed because Balthazar was fucking you so hard, but when I started thrusting into Knight, fuck. He was a bitch in heat, he looked like he was about to come before we'd even started. I could hardly hold myself off, I didn't want to be rough with him. But then, he begged me to. I saw it in his eyes, he wanted it hard and fast, he wanted me to fuck the come out of him."

A whimper escaped my throat, hearing his words and watching him jack himself off. God, I couldn't take this. I needed him to fuck me. Hoping it might help, I shut my eyes so I couldn't see him, but he kept talking.

"So I stopped holding myself back, I piston fucked his tight ass, I've never fucked a man that hard before. I fucked him until he shot his load all over me. It got on my chest, my hair. And then I came inside his ass so hard, I swear I almost passed out."

My pussy was so wet, it dripped all down my bound legs, and they started shaking from the effort of holding me up.

"Look at me." I opened my eyes and saw Arthur had undressed, exposing every curve and valley I'd spent many nights exploring with my mouth. "You're dripping onto the carpet. I've never seen a woman get so turned on during a story about me fucking her lover, but I knew it would have this effect on you. Next time I tie you up, I'm going to fuck him in front of you until he comes all over your naked body. Would you like that?" My timid yes was barely audible. I was beyond arousal, I was a puddle of need. Just touch me, flick me, anything.

I gasped in relief when he moved finally and jumped when his hands massaged my ass again. He pulled my cheeks apart and a fresh stream of wet escaped me, running down my legs to the floor where I felt a wet spot under my feet.

"That's what I want," he teased, making me shudder and more streams came from me as he massaged my ass more, kneading like it was made of dough. God, I hoped I didn't orgasm from it, but I was so close I had no idea what would set me off. He lifted his hands, I waited, and I felt the head of his cock push into my ass. I groaned in disappointment, I needed him in my pussy, I needed something to touch me there where I was throbbing with want. "You don't want me to fuck your ass?" I groaned again, but he cracked his hand across my ass cheek and I jumped away from him. "I'm going to fuck your ass like I fucked Knight's. I think you want that very much." He stopped playing nice, as if he was at all before, and he thrust inside until his balls slapped against my slit, splashing the wetness there. He interrupted my gasp, pulling on my hair until my back was arched so much, my breasts weren't touching the desk anymore. Then he started fucking me, the office filling with the wet slapping noise from his testicles hitting my body. Every few thrusts my clitoris got hit and I was about to come so hard. My moans tipped him off and he sped up, going in and out of me like a jackhammer. "Tell me when you're coming," he ordered, just as I knew it was going to happen. I could hardly breathe, much less speak.

"I'm..." He tugged on my hair and I started to climax, the wet sounds from me intensifying and the puddle growing on the floor. "I'm coming, oh god, fuck." His pace never slowed from the beginning of my orgasm until I'd stopped shuddering. My body was primed and it was not satisfied yet, easily throwing me close to another release. Arthur moved back so his balls weren't hitting me anymore and it made the climb that much harder with nothing to stimulate me except his ravenous fucking. What I thought would be an easy ascent turned into me trying desperately to climax but unable to get there. He fucked me like that for what felt like an hour and I was so frustrated I couldn't take it.

"Please, Arthur, please let me come again," I pleaded brokenly.

"That's it, baby. That's what I wanted."

Such an ass.

He pulled out and untied me, my limbs prickly as the feeling came back to them. Turning me, he lifted me up onto the desk and laid me out on it, lifting my legs and sliding back inside my ass.

"Rub your clit, come for me." I needed no other instruction, I put my hand between us and rubbed at my sensitive nub, his fucking picking up speed again until he was shoving me across the wood with every thrust.

"Oh…" I whined. "God yes, fuck me harder, make me…" I finally crested after so long, and loud guttural moans escaped me, my walls pulsing on his cock over and over. He kept going, kept fucking, until I came again not a minute later. He'd had his fun, and god it was some of the best sex I'd ever had. Even with my body still shaking, I sat up and kissed his lips, his rapid fucking jostling our lips together. "Come in my ass," I begged him, and he lost his control in an instant, thrusting and shooting his load inside me, grunting, gripping my hips so hard he was going to leave a bruise. He finally slowed and heaved, trying to catch his breath, leaning his head against my shoulder. His hands trembled slightly, but he picked me up, keeping us connected, and walked to the couch where he found a blanket to wrap around us, and he carried me naked up to my rooms where we fell asleep still entwined.

***

SOME TIME in the early morning, I was stirred in my sleep with Arthur's hand stroking my lower belly. I turned my head towards him, eyes still closed in a sleepy haze, and my hand found his bare chest, tickling the sparse, blonde hair there.

"Did I hurt you?" he asked in a whisper, though we were alone so there was no need to stay quiet.

I opened my eyes, only to see loving concern all over his scarred face. The sight of it nearly brought me to tears. "Of course not. Why would you think that?"

He dipped his head to my breast, squeezing his eyes shut tightly. "I know I can be intense. I don't ever want you to be afraid of me."

My heart melted, ached for him. I brought his head up to see the deep emotion on his face. "You've never told me that before." Something passed between us as we stared in each other's eyes, a vulnerability I'd never seen from the stoic icy warrior. Maybe I'd done something in my old life to stop him from being this exposed with me, or maybe he'd felt like he had to be strong for me and couldn't show me how he really felt.

I'd never felt so in love with him.

"Kiss me," I beckoned to him, folding him into me when he hovered over my body, gently kissing my lips, worshipping them with his mouth like they held the secrets to happiness. He kissed down my neck, burning my skin with every touch. Nestled between my legs, it was only a quick movement before he pushed his hardness inside me, and he started a slow, deep pace, rocking me into the bed as gently as possible.

From his position on top of me, I was free to stare right into his eyes, only breaking the contact to lift my head for a tender kiss. His hands trailed down my sides, massaging my skin, dipping back down to kiss as much of my chest and stomach that he could reach. We rocked together, no movement too hurried or desperate.

Slowly, my body was responding to his love making, and he reached between us, twirling his fingers around my nub, bending back on top of me to capture my lips in his. Gasping against his lips, I moaned and felt myself cresting, almost there. He kissed my breath away, his hand fisting into the sheet when he felt me tip over and I came, grasping at him as I shuddered and fell apart. The rhythm of his thrusts broke when he moaned his own release against my lips, falling against me with shaking limbs. With passion flooding over me, I stroked at his sweaty forehead, pushing his blonde hair out of the way.

"I love you, Lisbeth. If I can be happy about one thing in all this, it's that I didn't have to wait so long to possess you this time. It would've driven me mad."

I grinned a tired smile. "I don't think you liked me as quickly last time."

"Bullshit. I knew the moment I saw you that you belonged to me."

That made me giggle, bouncing him on my stomach. "That's a little awkward considering you still hunted me after said moment and arrested me, then kept me in my room for six months under house arrest. What do you call that?"

"Foreplay," he answered, like it was obvious.

The front door of my suite opened and we both sat up as Knight came into the bedroom, looking a little dirty and very exhausted. I was up in an instant, coming close to inspect him under the grit on his skin. He had a nasty cut on his leg somewhere, I could smell the blood on him.

"You should've let me come with you," I fussed, my heart falling at the sight of his blank face, dead tired from his run.

Arthur was there, taking his hand and leading him away from the door. "Let's get you cleaned up." We brought him to the bathroom and Arthur gently undressed him while I ran a bath in my large tub. When it was full enough, I stepped in first, already naked, and was there to help guide Knight to the middle of the water.

Arthur joined on Knight's other side, already soaping up a loofah and running it along Knight's arm. I got out my nail brush and we got to work on him like he was at a spa. When I switched to his feet and Arthur lifted his leg to inspect the healing cut, Knight started giggling at me, making me pause in my work.

"What?" I asked, bending to run the nail brush on his toes.

"You two fuss over me like I'm a toddler who can't clean his own feet."

I squinted and splashed at him before Arthur took Knight's neck in his hand and they shared a passionate kiss while I watched from Knight's feet. "It's because you're exhausted, and we love you." They stopped, realizing Arthur hadn't said that to Knight before now. "I love you," he clarified, kissing the werewolf again, as tenderly as he had with me. Too tired for more, Arthur leaned against the back of the tub, taking Knight with him until he lay across the vampire's chest. I swam up to them and joined in, putting my head on the crook of Knight's neck, and Arthur's arms went up around me, holding us both in his protective embrace.

13

RED FLAG

*fter leaving Knight to rest for a few hours, Arthur and I went hand in hand down to my office to finish my work from the night before. Anastasia was already there, perched on the edge of my desk, in the exact spot where Arthur had taken me. Thankfully the spot on the carpet had dried, but my cheeks still flushed as I walked past her and I knew Arthur was chuckling to himself.

"Where's Lucas and Clara?" I asked her as I picked up the notes and my marker.

She answered without looking up from her journal. "They're fucking."

I whirled on her, turning even more pink. "Mom! What the hell?!"

Her apathetic shrug only made it worse. "Not like you weren't doing it earlier. I can smell it all over this room." She

186

peered over her book, giving Arthur a knowing glance. "Better be treating my daughter right. You're all she has if the witch's prediction is true."

"Knight isn't going to die, mom. Don't say that, I can't handle it. You know how I feel about losing him."

Her apathy turned into sympathy. "I know, baby. Why do you think I went comatose for centuries? I lost my mate too, and then I lost you. I know exactly what you're feeling. That's why I won't rest until we stop Alistair so we can get our future back as much as possible." She paused, and the tight look on her face told me she'd been effected by my story about Marie much more than I'd thought. She would never get to fall in love with the woman who had made her happy in my time. It passed as soon as it came, and she was back to her journal, making a few notes with a pencil on the yellowed pages.

I went back to the board, marking more spots off the map with black circles, and lines showing where Anastasia had journeyed in her search. Arthur was busying himself with phone calls in one corner of the room, trying to figure out what the other Orders were doing after the death of the Council. I was so engrossed with my work on the map, I hardly noticed he wasn't beside me until his hands were suddenly on my sides and I jumped forward in surprise. He was studying the board intensely when I stared up at him, trying to see anything I hadn't found yet.

"Christ, this is pointless," Anastasia declared, throwing the book down onto the carpet and pushing off the desk in frustration. "It took me almost fifty years to find him the first time. There's no guarantee he'll even be in the same hideout. He has dozens, hundreds of them. Look at this." She gestured to the map in front of us that had so many black dots and lines, it was almost completely covered in them.

"Well, last time he knew you were hunting him, no thanks to the traitor we still need to find. This time he feels safe so he'll pick a spot that he knows we won't look at. One that he knows we'll never..." I trailed off, a thought forming when I noticed one of the only spots on the map still unmarked. My office door opened, interrupting my thoughts when I smelled Knight's scent.

My mate was standing in my office with the Lycan, Alexander, beside him. Olivier was fast approaching in the hall and she looked like she was about to murder someone.

"*You!*" she shrieked at Knight, leveling him with her rage when he looked back at her. "You brought a *Lycan* into my house. You're lucky I'm not allowed to touch you, *boy*, because you're in deep shit now." Her rage went from a fifteen to a one when I signaled for her to back down, and she meekly took a step away, still shooting daggers at Knight as she went.

"While Olivier is correct," Arthur started, and I glared at him until he held out a hand for me to wait. "We are trying to make peace with the Lycans, so it's not like we didn't reach out first. Despite the current laws, you are welcome and safe here." Olivier grumbled under her breath and tightly crossed her arms over her chest. One of us was getting an earful later, probably me for not controlling my boyfriends well enough.

With Anastasia pacing the floor, we showed Alexander to one of the various couches in my large office, and the vampires sat across from the wolves.

"So," I started, my attention drawing briefly to my mother's pacing. "You got Arthur's message that we wanted to talk?"

"Actually, Knight came to see us last night," he answered, and we looked at our mate in surprise.

Knight's sheepish look was quickly replaced with a resolved one. "I figured they would respond better to our plan if I spoke to them first. I held off my shift until we were done talking, and then I ran all night to make up for it. His pack came with me to watch, just to show them... that I'm not dangerous." His brief look where I sat said he still didn't fully believe it, but the fact that he'd made such an effort that could've gone so wrong left me speechless. He'd trusted me that much.

Arthur wasn't knocked speechless, however, because he let his opinion of the matter fly freely. "That was stupid of you. Any number of things could've happened."

Knight inhaled deeply, his eyes narrowing at the vampire, but clearly holding back his retort since we were in mixed company. "It worked. Alexander is willing to negotiate a cease fire for his pack. We're hoping to spread it around until the other packs are on board as well."

"Knight's willingness to speak with us at the risk of his

life wasn't the only thing we had to consider," Alexander started. He turned his eyes to me. "It was what you said to me when you spared the boy. I had to question why I'd been taught to hate your kind, and why you'd been taught to hate mine. This bracelet," he said, holding his wrist up so his vampire teeth bracelet could jangle freely. "This wasn't mine. It's been handed down in my pack for a very long time. I tell you honestly I've never put a single tooth on here. I've never killed one of your kind, nor has anyone in my pack. When I realized that, I wondered why, if we weren't even fighting anymore, why we had to keep doing it. When Knight came asking for peace for our enemies, it was clear he felt the same."

"It wasn't an easy sell," Knight added. "But they were willing to listen, after Alexander told them what you did for the boy."

"If you lift the kill order on us, we'll lift ours on you."

I held out a hand for Alexander to shake. "Done. Consider us allies again. If you need anything, we'll be there for you."

The Lycan pumped my hand and smiled warmly, the way he did in my other life. "Speaking of which, Knight has told me about this vampire Alistair. He was a bit mum on some of the details, but if this man has killed your leaders, I think you could use some allies, and since you've got us on your side now, we'd be honored to fight alongside you if it comes to that."

The memory of his dead body stopped me cold. He died for me once. I didn't want him to do that again.

Arthur was quick to accept as I'd lost the ability to answer. "I can't think of a better pack to be by our sides. Thank you, Alexander." The men all stood up and Olivier led Alexander back out with Anastasia following behind. As soon as I couldn't hear their voices, Knight went up to the office doors to shut them.

"Arthur, why would do you that?" I asked him in disbelief. "You know he died for us in my time. I don't want him anywhere near this battle."

Before I could finish my tirade, Knight slammed the doors and whirled on Arthur so fast he was a blur. "Who in the *fuck* do you think you are?" he demanded, approaching the vampire so fast Arthur actually backed up one step before standing still. "*'That was stupid of you?'* You have no fucking right to treat me like a child. Last night was beautiful and sweet, and I love that you take care of me, but I'm not a toddler you have to admonish when I step out of line. I'm a grown man, I make my own choices, and if I want to do something that's a little risky, that's my decision, not yours." The two men faced off, Knight standing several inches higher so Arthur had to tilt his head up to stare into his eyes. "You might think I'm just going to let you do whatever you want because I let you fuck me, but it's about time someone took you down a notch."

Ahh fuck me.

I expected an instant passionate, erotic kiss, but Knight wasn't finished.

"Tell me what you did to Lisbeth while I was out," he ordered, sounding exactly like the Knight I'd known in my time, commanding and strong. God, it was so hot.

Arthur swallowed hard, trying desperately to hold himself together. "I fucked her. Twice."

"You're going to have to be more detailed than that. She had bruises on her hips."

Was he mad? Did he think Arthur had injured me? I stood and interjected, just in case. "He didn't hurt me, I asked him to do it."

Knight took his eyes from Arthur for one second, and that was all I needed to know he wasn't upset. He was winding our lover up. "I said tell me."

Arthur's jaw worked several times before he answered. "I tied her hands behind her back, then I tied her legs together and bent her naked over the desk." Without breaking their stare, Knight reached between them and started undoing Arthur's pants, almost making him falter in his words. "I stood where she could see me, stroking my cock for her and telling her what it was like to fuck you, to have you mewling underneath me and begging for more. She started dripping onto the floor, it made her so wet."

Slipping under Arthur's waistband, Knight gripped his erection firmly, moving his hand up and down with their eyes locked. "Keep talking."

"I fucked her ass until she came for me. Then I fucked her

hard for so long, making sure she couldn't have a second orgasm because I wanted her to beg me for it. When she'd had enough, she begged for me to make her come. I untied her and put her on her back, fucking her and rubbing her clit until she came again, screaming out every shudder." He swallowed again once he was done, a gasp almost escaping his lips over the hand job Knight was giving him.

"Lisbeth," Knight said, his other hand pulling on Arthur's jeans and boxers until they fell to the ground, and he brought his hand around to grasp one of Arthur's ass cheeks, massaging it in time with his other hand. "I assume the restraints are still in here?" I nodded and walked on wobbly legs to where I'd stashed them earlier, before he could ask me to like I knew he would. I brought the ties to them and Knight had just removed Arthur's shirt, exposing his body completely to us. "Tie his hands back." I did so, pulling his thick arms behind his body and securing them enough where I was certain even he couldn't escape. Not that he wanted to, I was sure. "If I was super pissed at you, I'd make you walk up to our rooms like this," Knight mused, an evil glint in his eye that was making me so fucking wet. "But instead, I'm just going to fuck you. I'm going to take you harder than you've ever taken a cock before. I'm going to fuck the come out of you. The only way you're going to climax is from my cock inside you. As soon as I stop touching your dick, neither Lisbeth nor myself will touch it again until we're finished."

God, fuck this. I was burning up like an inferno and they

were about to fuck, meaning they'd be too busy for me. This would've been the perfect opportunity for Balthazar to pop in and just screw me as I watched my lovers fucking, but he was still gone and I was dying from arousal. Sensing my needs, Knight motioned for me to follow as he led Arthur by his cock to a different couch, the very one I'd been sitting on when Arthur first kissed me.

"Get undressed," Knight told me, his hand firmly stroking Arthur as they watched me take my shirt and pants off, flinging my panties off last, then I sat on the cold leather couch and waited. "Get between her legs, you're going to eat her pussy while I fuck you. If she's not screaming, I'll stop and give *her* my cock instead." He helped Arthur kneel and I spread my legs wide, almost trembling when the icy vampire's mouth came closer and closer to my exposed center. "Make her come first, then I'll fuck you."

Arthur dove in, his tongue running up my wet labia, flicking out the tip of it to lap at my clitoris. A cry came out of me before I knew I was making it when my lover sucked my nub between his lips and wiggled it back and forth until my eyes rolled into the back of my head. Knight was there, kissing me roughly and bringing his hands up to twist my nipples. I was too turned on, too heated, too ready, it only took a few seconds until I came on Arthur's face and whimpered against Knight's lips for more. The restraint he had fell for one moment when he leaned his head against my cheek.

I want to fuck you all day and all night, Lisbeth, he sent to my mind, already more attuned to me than my other lovers.

You smell so amazing right now, I'm not sure what it is, but it's driving me insane.

I was almost brought out of the haze because Knight had said the very same thing to me when I was expecting Jason, and again with Gwen. The pregnancy potion worked, but I should've been expecting Kitty first. Arthur interrupted me contemplating going back to ask the witches about it by sticking his tongue inside my pussy and thrusting it in and out of me.

Throwing my head back and almost falling over, Knight left me with another kiss and knelt behind Arthur, positioning himself at the right spot to massage the vampire's ass, pulling his cheeks apart. I could hardly tell whether the noises Arthur was making were from licking me or from the feeling of Knight rubbing the head of his cock against Arthur's tight rosebud. He pushed in and as Arthur was unable to steady himself with his hands tied behind his back, he pushed further into me, my ass sliding across the leather couch seat.

"God, he feels so good, Lisbeth," Knight moaned out, stopping for a moment to control himself, then he cracked his hand across Arthur's ass. "She's not screaming. Do you want me to stop?"

Arthur's tongue was a blur on me, slurping up every drop of my arousal, and a very apparent moan escaped his mouth as Knight started slowly pushing in and out of him, momentarily bringing him away from me. His short hair didn't leave me much to work with in the way of grabbing onto him, so I wrapped a hand around the back of his head and pushed him until he resumed his task.

Knight had just started speeding his thrusts up when I felt the tension rising inside me. I went back and forth between shoving Arthur's head on my clit and trying to pull him away when I got too sensitive.

"Show him what you need," Knight told me, meeting my eyes and holding them, slapping against Arthur's hips. "Connect your heads, but don't let him feel your pleasure. I want to know when he's about to come."

I did exactly that, connecting us at such a small level that I could feel his level of arousal and urgency like a meter, and he could feel the same for me. He used the information expertly, like he'd been doing this for years, and he started alternating between licking my nub or around it depending on my sensitivity. I was climbing again, this time slower but evenly with him paying attention to when I couldn't take it and when I wanted more. God, he'd never been this skilled before. Maybe I should've started doing this a long time ago.

That thought ended because I hit a point and even though I was too stimulated, he never stopped sucking me into his mouth, and I screamed out an orgasm that made me grab the back of the couch to stay upright.

"That's it," Knight approved in a husky whisper. Like he'd finally earned it, Knight started fucking Arthur as hard as I'd been fucked the night before, at a pace that had me breathless just from watching it. My connection to Arthur had all sorts of things coming to me, how much he liked Knight's cock, how he'd never taken one that big before, and god it felt good. He wanted to climax but he was going to hold off for as long as possible so he could be fucked longer. He just wanted Knight to keep his dick inside him, even if it meant never letting go.

He was still trying to retain control, even tied up and helpless between his lovers, and I wasn't going to allow it.

I straightened, pushing his head up and sitting forward on the couch until his face was level with mine. "How long have you wanted Knight's cock inside you?" I asked him, putting my lips a breath away from his and I could see him straining to close the distance and kiss me. His ragged breath was hot on my face, the scent of my arousal on his lips thick and intoxicating. I wanted to lick all of it up, but I had to focus on him since he still hadn't answered me. He'd hardly spoken this whole time, when before he'd been a chatterbox trying to make me so aroused I about died from it.

"Answer her, Arthur," Knight piped up, mid-fuck. A steady sheen of sweat was forming on his tanned skin, I wanted to lick it more than I wanted to lick Arthur's face.

The vampire inhaled deeply, a haze of arousal coming over his icy eyes. "Since I first saw him in that bathroom only wearing a towel. I wanted to fuck him, I wanted him to fuck me. It was impossible to decide which one I wanted first. I only knew I needed him as desperately as I needed you."

I almost kissed him, so overcome with need that I wanted him back between my legs, but I held off and pushed him up slightly, Knight assisting me by pulling Arthur's tied arms back until he was arched in front of me, exposing his muscled chest. "I'll tell you a secret," I said huskily, running one finger from his throat down to his sternum. "One time the other Knight and I tied you like this, and he fucked you while I watched. You begged for one of us to touch your cock, anything to make you climax, but we refused, and you held off so we wouldn't get what we wanted, like you're doing now. Only the other you forgot one thing about you that we knew."

"Shit, what was it?" Knight asked me, enthralled with the story and his rapid thrusting.

Instead of saying it out loud, I leaned down and sucked one of Arthur's taut nipples into my mouth, and he howled like a bitch in heat against us, Knight on one end and me on the other. My hand reached and tweaked his other nipple, making him moan a chorus of ecstasy, and the connection between us lit up like a Christmas tree.

Unwilling to take my mouth off his nipple, I sent the thought to Knight. *He's about to come, keep going.* Impossibly, Knight's thrusts got even faster until Arthur's control slipped so far he went over and Knight fucked the come out of him in spurts that landed on my naked body, wave after wave until he went limp and Knight let him go so he crashed into my lap, heaving and moaning. With his hands gripping Arthur's hips tightly, Knight kept fucking our lover, his groaning turning more erotic by the second, signaling his impending climax. I got up, gently putting Arthur's head onto the couch, and approached Knight, planting myself against the back of his sweaty body. I ran my hands up the globes of his ass and squeezed them, enjoying the way it made him twitch forward.

I sat up on my heels and caught the edge of his ear between my teeth. "Come for us, baby," I whispered to him, bringing my hands up to flick across his nipples. The trick wasn't the same for him, but he still responded, and his hips jerked when his pleasure heightened and he slammed his come into Arthur's ass, growling it out like a madman possessed.

It was so unbelievably hot.

The werewolf wobbled, falling to the side to collapse on the carpet, only for Arthur to do the same a moment later, sliding off the couch until they were lying together, drained and catching their breath. Mid-gasps, Knight untied the bonds on Arthur's wrists and they reached for the other's hand, clasping them together between their bodies. Once his chest was rising at a normal speed, Knight turned his face to the side so he could study Arthur's chiseled profile.

"*I love you,* Arthur," he said gently, in complete contrast with his intense fucking, but so him it melted my heart.

Arthur turned his face over and a genuine smile came to his lips as he stared at his lover. He brought one of his large hands up and stroked Knight's cheek, leaning close for a tender kiss. "You'd better," he whispered against Knight's lips. "Because it would be a bit awkward if you didn't, considering how much I love you." They rested their foreheads together in a loving embrace. "I'm sorry I disrespected you. I don't ever want you to feel belittled by me."

A squeak came from me when I put my fists to my mouth, ruining the moment and turning both of them towards where I still sat on the carpet, staring like a drooling idiot.

Knight tossed his chin at me. "Get over here." I happily did, lying between them, cuddling into Arthur's body and holding Knight up to mine so I could kiss his lips over and over.

WITH ARTHUR DOWN more than a few notches, we went back to the board and Knight was just pulling his shirt over his head when there was a knock on the locked doors. Arthur opened it and Anastasia strolled in like this was a normal day.

"That was tedious. I had to wait for you to finish and there wasn't anything for me to do except look at every book in the library here. I've read half of them already. Is there anything in there that wasn't published over three hundred years ago?"

Arthur straightened his shirt only to discover it was on backwards and he tried fixing it where my mom wouldn't see. "Sorry about that. The making you wait part, not the books."

She shrugged and went back to her perch on my desk,

face in her journal. "If the sex doesn't take at least half an hour it's not worth doing."

"*Mom!*" I shrieked, turning beet red.

"You get so upset when I mention your sex life. Were you this uptight before, or is that new?"

"I had kids in the house before now, so no, I wasn't always saying out loud how bomb their dicks are and how they make me pass out when I orgasm."

That brought her up over the top of her journal, eyebrow raised with interest. "The kids aren't here yet, I'd love to hear this story in depth. Right now."

"*NO!*"

After threatening to throw the box of tacks at her, she went back to her notes and I sat on the floor looking up at the board, trying to pick up that thought again that I'd had before. There were only a few spots on the map without marks, and one was staring out at me like a sore thumb. It was so obvious, I felt like the dumbest person on the planet when I stood up and walked closer to confirm my suspicions. Everyone else noticed, stopping what they were doing to look at me.

"Babe, what's up?" Knight asked me, getting up from the coffee table.

I held a hand out for Arthur to give me one of the sharpies, and when he did, I uncapped it and reached up on my tiptoes to draw a giant circle around England, then I pointed to it with the pen. "He's there."

Anastasia came to stand beside me. "How do you know?"

"It's where my Order used to live, the very place where we abandoned Alistair and the other turned vampires when we moved here in the 1800's. They mentioned it before in my time, how much it made them hate us. What better place to stay than one we would never look at?"

"The castle is still standing?" Arthur asked, crossing over to one of the cabinets behind my desk and opening a drawer to flip through the documents inside.

"I think so. We technically still own it, we just moved out. I bet Othello kept it just in case we had to come back. I haven't been there in..." I raised my eyebrows, thinking back to the day so long ago when I left my home and childhood behind. "Three hundred years."

"I thought you left in the 1800's?" Knight asked, doing the math in his head.

I waved the marker at him absently. "I was off with Olivier for a century, fucking prostitutes and seducing debutantes."

Arthur stopped for a second, looking up at me with curiosity about that last bit, but he went back to the papers until he produced the one he was looking for and brought it to us. "The deed to the castle, it's still there."

I took it when he was close enough and scanned the page. "Looks like there's a grounds keeper, or there's an assigned one, at least. I don't know how much grounds keeping he can do when he's..." My heart stopped and I looked up with horror. Meeting Arthur's eyes, I turned the paper around and held it out to him, putting my finger at the spot that changed everything. "Estinien is the grounds keeper."

"So?" he said, not getting it yet.

"Estinien can't be the grounds keeper of my Order's castle. He's the head of his own Order so he'd never do such a menial task, not to mention he lives in Australia. There's no way he'd travel there for upkeep unless he had a reason." Anger pooled inside me, so intense I saw red. "He's been under my nose this whole time, in this time and the other one, playing me like a fiddle and ruining the world like it meant nothing to him when he stood by our side and fought with us like he gave a shit. *God damn him.*" I emphasized my anger by kicking the board over and it slammed into the carpet, spreading tacks everywhere. "I'm going to wrap my hands around his throat until he stops breathing, and then I'll burn his filthy corpse piece by piece as I rip off his limbs."

"Red flag," Knight whispered in the silence that followed my tirade.

I felt no shame. Only rage.

"I'm not trusting a single person outside of this family and Olivier. Estinien might've been at the head, but we don't know how many of us were part of this, and if Alistair knows we're coming, we're dead in the water. Arthur, make sure Renard and Cameron are taken to safety, I don't trust them around us since they're still human. When you're back, I have another mission if we can spare someone." He was off without another word, my dutiful soldier. "You," I said, pointing the pen to Knight. "We need to clue in my other parents and make sure they're either coming or going, I don't want them here either because Clara is human. It would be ideal for them to stay with Renard and Cameron, but I don't trust my father with people he doesn't know. He might drain them in their sleep because they smelled like pea soup."

"A wise choice," my mother noted beside me, watching Knight leave after I was done. "You're quite the leader. They don't even question you, they just hop off to obey. I don't know how you won them over to you so quickly, it's like, and I say this ironically considering the circumstances, there's magic at play."

I smiled, looking down at the floor. "In the other time, they used to insist they would've fallen in love with me no matter how we met. I thought they were wrong, but it seems they were correct."

"Do you miss them?" she asked, surprising me.

"They've been gone for five seconds, I'm fine."

"Not these versions of them, the other ones. The ones that you spent so many years with. The Knight you married, the Arthur you longed for for so long before finally having him in your arms. The men you have now aren't the same ones you left."

"Maybe not," I conceded, and I let the question wash over me until I was sure of my answer. "Only... Last night, Arthur told me something he's never said to me before. Not in sixty-seven years. And Knight has never been this open in front of me. He told me he thought Balthazar was hot, he's never said something like that before. Of course I'll miss the men I spent so much time with, but..." I sighed and held myself with my arms. "It's still them. They're still with me. I'll always carry those memories, they'll never fade, and that means neither will the other versions of the men I love."

"Hmm," she said quietly, contemplating me like she usually did before she responded.

Arthur returned, coming up to me and kissing my forehead before reporting. "Renard and Cameron are off, they're going to spend time with your former companion, Galen. His vineyard should be safe." I nodded in agreement. After all this was over, I'd have to spend some time with Galen and tell him about everything I'd been through. He'd been dead for a long time in my old timeline, seeing him again would make me very happy. "What was the mission you needed?" he asked, bringing me out of my head.

"Right, that. I need someone to go find Knight's sister. If Alistair starts recruiting turned vampires, hoping not, her rogue coven might be in danger. Last time all of her friends were killed, she didn't take too kindly to us after that. I'd rather Knight never go through seeing her that hurt. If someone could go find them and keep them safe, I'd be grateful."

"Actually," Arthur started, making me raise my eyebrows at him. "I've found someone you might be interested in seeing. Ever since you told me the names of vampires we knew, I've been on the lookout for them. Some aren't born yet, but I had a bit of luck a few days ago."

I wiggled a finger at him with a squint. "I'm not liking this constant secret keeping you've got going on for dramatic effect. Can we shelve that personality trait?"

He glared at me, almost looking like he wanted to roll his eyes. "Do you want to see or not?"

"Fine, whatever, let's go."

He led me outside the office and I felt something in the pit of my stomach when we got closer, something I'd felt a long time ago when Knight suddenly appeared in a crowd before me, not quite as dead as I'd thought.

Standing in the foyer was a gangly teenager, looking barely old enough to have a driver's license. He was staring up at the ceiling with his mouth wide open and I didn't recognize him until he turned and look right at me.

Dominic.

He'd been Kitty's mate in the future, the boy with the blonde hair and the duel-toned eyes, one blue and one brown. He looked so young, so vulnerable looking. I'd known him as a man capable of protecting my daughter. This version of him made me want to check his temperature and put him to bed early.

He grinned warmly at me, also something different for him, and launched off in his Australian accent. "How ya goin'? You must be the sheila Arthur was banging on about. I'm Dom." He held his hand out for me to shake and I didn't miss him trying to look at my chest when he thought I wasn't paying attention. Arthur turned rigid, noticing a few vampires coming into the foyer to see who was talking so loudly, and he led us back into my office for some privacy, shutting and locking the doors behind us. Dom raised his eyebrows at Arthur flipping the locks but he didn't comment on it.

"Sorry," I said to him, resisting the very powerful urge to hug him. "We don't know who to trust right now."

Turning, Arthur got right to it, no foreplay or anything. "We believe your leader Estinien is a traitor."

Dom laughed, which wasn't the reaction I was expecting. "If you're trying to put the wind up me, you're gonna have to do better than that. Estinien's a seriously dodgy bloke. What do you want me to do?"

Arthur's skeptical eyebrow raise was monumental. "As my leader said, we don't know who to trust right now. You're one of the few we do, so we'd like to recruit you to be a Hunter."

"Whoa, a vampire Hunter? Noice." He stopped, realizing something I knew he'd bring up. "But we've never met before. You don't know me from a bar of soap, how can you tell if I'm a fair dinkum or not?"

"I've heard good things about you from your Order," I said without missing a beat. "We've been in contact with them since the Council was killed, and your name came up several times." Dom looked like I'd just made his day, like no one had ever believed in him before. He straightened his jacket with a large grin on his face.

"Your first mission as a Hunter will be finding a rogue vampire coven and protecting them if a threat comes."

"Epic!" Dom responded in excitement.

Arthur got out the paperwork to make Dom an official Hunter and eyed the teenager walking about my office, commenting on just about everything he could see. "You're sure about him?" he asked, handing me a pen to sign the papers. "He looks like he's never even kissed a girl. I'm not sure I'd trust him to watch an egg."

I elbowed my lover and leaned over to sign the contract. "He's just young. He's going to grow into a fine man, just you wait. You trusted him with my daughter's life before, I know you wouldn't have done that lightly."

Leaning in to kiss my temple, he deferred to my wisdom by letting Dom put his signature on the papers, but I could see him grumbling about it internally. The fact he was shutting his mouth at all spoke volumes. I waited until Dom had left before I slowly approached Arthur, running a single finger up his bicep.

"It's terrifyingly sexy when you do what I say," I purred, waiting for him to stop straightening the papers before planting myself against him.

He looked down at me, fire and ice on his scarred face. "Time and place, love of my life. We literally just had sex."

Grinning, I stood up on my tip toes and nuzzled our noses together. "Maybe I want you again." Our lips joined in a kiss full of longing, only interrupted with someone coming into the office.

"I leave for five minutes and you're already making out."

Knight came up behind me, hopped up onto my desk, and held me against him so we were both facing our lover.

"We have to rally our troops," Arthur said, a flicker of heat remaining on his face even though he was trying to be all business now. "Since most of the vampires here are too soft, present company…" He debated on how he was going to finish his phrase, either implying I was a weakling or admitting I was at his level.

"I kicked your ass before, choose that word wisely," I reminded him with a raised eyebrow.

"…excluded," he finished, almost rolling his eyes. "Keep quiet, I'm planning. That means we have to rally the Hunters and anyone else who is qualified. Olivier is bringing them all here but it might take time, especially considering we can't let anyone know we're doing it."

Knight's hand slipped beneath my shirt and he started massaging my breast, making sure Arthur could see. "We could meet on the Lycan reservation. None of the vampires would go there willingly yet."

Arthur noted that with an appreciative glance and got his phone out to text someone. "That's good, that will work fine. Good thinking, umm…" He trailed off and started looking a little red.

"You were going to say 'love' weren't you?" I teased with a wide smile.

He narrowed his eyes at me and went back to the texting. "Shut up, your teasing is going to get you in trouble."

"Not like I've never been punished for it before," I countered, meeting his eyes as Knight's hand squeezed my breast, but we both broke off into giggles under Arthur's stare and couldn't keep it up.

Despite our immaturity, the corner of his mouth lifted and I could've sworn he was trying not to laugh. "You two are something else, I swear. I've never seen a couple more alike in my life. It's no wonder you fought so hard to get him back."

We both erupted in cutsie baby noises that ran Arthur out of the office before we could finish our meeting.

14

THE BATTLE FOR OUR FUTURE

*A*fter several days of covert planning, we were just arriving at the Lycan reservation, ready for our army to join us. Though we were now at peace with the pack, not everyone we passed looked happy about it, and we met more than a few rude looks before Alexander appeared at their meeting hall with a welcoming smile.

"Arthur, Knight," he said in greeting. "We've set up the hall if you two would like to make sure everything is in order." They went up to the door, turning when I stayed behind. "Lisbeth, I'd like you to come meet someone." We followed him inside the meeting hall, and I marveled for a second time at the tall, vaulted ceiling made of beautiful, raw wood.

Standing in the middle of the room was Simon and his

parents. Both of them were hesitant as we approached, but they tried to keep their faces polite.

Alexander stood between us and held out a hand to me. "Simon, this is Lisbeth."

I stared down at the small boy in bittersweet wonderment. He still looked so much like my Jason.

"You're the vampire that saved me," he said with a smile.

"It's nice to meet you, Simon." I faltered, swallowing down tears that were trying to come out.

"Alexander says you're nice. He says you don't want us to fight anymore. Is that because of your son?" He'd remembered what I said to him at the crosswalk, but just hearing him say it made me long for my children that much more.

Knight pulled me against him, holding me close as I tried not to cry. Simon left with his parents soon after, but not before they stared at us in confusion, a werewolf and a vampire in love. Knight held me when the Hunters arrived and all through Arthur's strategy meeting, kissing my head and warming me right to my center.

With our plans made and everyone ready, we stayed at the reservation overnight to make sure the Hunters behaved themselves.

In the meeting hall amongst dozens of sleeping bags, I lay between two of my lovers, warmed from both sides. More than a few of the Hunters had been giving us dirty looks during the meeting, but Arthur silenced them all into submission so they wisely kept their comments to themselves.

"Is it weird I miss Balthazar?" Knight whispered with his lips against my forehead.

Arthur's arms tightened around me. "I do too. You're sure he doesn't like men, babe?"

"There is a reason for this reality to exist, and it's this conversation right here," I mused with a smile. "He can't get it up for a man. Incubi don't work like that."

"A shame," Arthur pouted, nibbling on my ear. "Maybe the Bicus can throw us a bone so then I can throw him a bone."

"Shut up, Arthur!" one of the Hunters complained loudly. "No one wants to hear about you boning an Incubus."

"The next person who talks will be babysitting Lisbeth's crazy dad," Arthur shouted, and the room went dead silent from the threat.

"You're so commanding, it's very sexy," Knight whispered, kissing Arthur above my head.

"Either fuck or get out, I'm trying to sleep," another complaint came from the room.

"Clarissa, you're on babysitting duty," Arthur declared, giving Knight another tender kiss.

"*God damn it!*"

OLIVIER WOKE us up the next morning, clattering around with a trunk that she slammed into the ground and unlocked, opening it out until the lid hit the floor. I was barely conscious but I could see her lifting out artillery and handing it to the vampires that were already awake, Arthur included. Knight sat up, stretched, and Arthur took a few seconds away from his gun to stare appreciatively as Olivier rolled her eyes at him.

I got up as well, stretching like a cat and flipping my hair back, keeping Arthur in my sights so I knew exactly how long he stood there gaping at me, then I turned and leaned against Knight, kissing him good morning.

"If you two are done cuddling, I have some stuff for you," Olivier threw out, not looking up from her task. I joined her and Arthur at the trunk while Knight changed his shirt. Olivier handed me a belt full of death giving toys. Two pistols and several knives were on it so I wrapped it around my waist and buckled it, pulling one of the guns out and inspecting it.

"You *can* shoot a gun, right?" Arthur asked as he watched me, so I glowered at him.

"This is the second time you've doubted my skills, Arthur. Let's not go for a third."

Knight approached wearing a shirt that had the words *'Alpha Kenny Body'* on the front. He also took his offered belt from Olivier and settled it on his hips to buckle it. "Where's my wooden stake?" All three of us stepped back to stare at him in complete disbelief. "Kidding. You should see your faces," he sniggered. "I'm assuming we're not taking a traditional plane since they won't let us keep these on board?"

"Alistair might know if we use one of our private jets, so

we're going to use someone else's," Olivier answered, closing her now empty trunk and standing with one of her pistols in her hands. "Lock and load, everyone. We're moving out."

Outside, we met my mother who already had her own equipment strapped to her waist, and it included a giant whip that she held in one hand. She followed beside me as we started leaving the reservation, only to be stopped by a group of Lycans with Alexander at the front.

"We want to come with you," he said firmly. "I know you don't want us to risk our lives for something that doesn't involve us, but we're allies now. If we can't be there when it counts, then I can't consider myself a true friend."

Arthur gave me a quick look before he stepped up and handed Alexander his spare pistol. "We'd be honored to fight alongside our brothers."

I swallowed my trepidation down like a choking hazard vitamin and pulled out my spare pistol, handing it to the Lycan beside Alexander. "Just watch your backs."

The Lycan smiled at me. "That's what you're here for."

With the extra numbers, we left the reservation and traveled across the forest until we reached the airport, just in case Alistair had eyes in town. Arthur signaled for us to wait at the edge of the airport gate and after a few minutes a human came over to us and opened the padlock on the metal gate doors. Our group moved across the runways, past several commercial planes until we found the one Arthur had hired for our journey, and everyone got on board. It was larger than our private jet, and it had just enough room for everyone.

Everyone buckled in and the plane took off, soaring through the sky to our destination. As soon as it was safe to get up, I took my seatbelt off and climbed into Knight's lap on the seat next to mine, cuddling against him and holding his face close to mine. The closer we got to Alistair, the closer we got to Sara's vision of Knight's death, and while I was determined to protect him at all costs, it loomed over me like a dagger, waiting to strike at any moment.

Eventually I was too worked up, and while everyone else was busy waiting out the long plane ride by watching a movie or reading something, I got up and walked to the back where the bathroom stalls were. One was empty and I stepped inside, shutting the door behind me and enclosing myself in the small space. I ran some water in the sink and splashed my face, looking at myself in the mirror. Of course I looked flawless, but I felt ragged and tired. If I actually looked it, it might've made me feel better about my mood. Or worse. Who knew?

I leaned against the wall, looking at my reflection, running a hand across my lower belly where a baby was growing, still a cluster of cells that didn't resemble a baby at all. It would be several weeks before I'd be able to hear her heartbeat, just to remind me she was really there.

"*Balzjanyóur nappnia lanliápob*," I said to the mirror, but Balthazar didn't appear. He was supposed to come when I said the words, no matter where he was.

Someone knocked on the bathroom stall and the door opened as I realized I hadn't locked it. Knight came in, shutting and locking the door behind him, his massive frame taking up most of the space, forcing me to jump up onto the sink counter.

"I heard you trying to call Balthazar," he said, coming up and putting his arms around me. He was so warm in the cold space, I held him as close as I could to warm me back up.

The more time that passed, the more my heart fell because the Incubus still hadn't appeared. "It didn't work. Maybe he's left for good."

Knight pulled my chin up so I could look into his eyes. "There is no way in hell he would abandon you."

"What if they put him in jail again? We'd have no way of knowing."

He leaned down and gave me a gentle kiss, making my insides flutter from his touch. "I promise after this if he's not back before our first baby is born, we'll all journey to the Bicus realm to find him. I don't care how much time it takes, we're not leaving one of our mates behind." He swept me up in another hug and I wished we weren't in such a public place. I needed him badly, just to reassure myself he was still there. We kissed and rested our foreheads together, breathing deeply and trying to still our racing hearts. "Stay by my side when we get there. Nothing can hurt me if you're there watching my back."

My chest was alive with love and pain, sorrow and happiness, passion and burning numbness, I felt like a madman trying to sort it all out, so I just clung to Knight and rode the waves as they came, dripping hot tears onto his shirt. We stood like that for at least half an hour before someone knocked on the door.

"If you two are done making out, I'd like to use the toilet." Knight picked me up, I wrapped my arms around his neck and he anchored me with his hands around me, only letting go briefly to unlock and open the bathroom door where we saw Olivier standing there with her hands on her hips. "I'm all for joining the mile high club, but people have to piss here," she smarted, gesturing behind her with her thumb where a few people had formed a line to the toilets.

My face reddening, Knight set me down and we walked back to our seats where I went back onto his lap. Arthur and I held hands across the walk space until I drooped against Knight's chest and fell asleep.

REFRESHED and ready after taking a long rest, I sprang up as soon as the plane landed and was the first to the door, dragging Knight behind me as he rubbed his sleepy eyes.

"Always eager," Arthur noted dryly, coming up behind us. He threaded his fingers through Knight's other hand and we waited for the steps to be brought over and the attendant to open the plane door, then we were off and out as fast as possible.

Bypassing the human rules and regulations, we'd landed

in a private airport owned by one of Arthur's many contacts, and waiting for us was a fleet of camouflage army jeeps. A man wearing a matching camo outfit stood by the vehicles and saluted when we approached.

"Which one is ours, General Lancaster?" I asked my lover with a cheeky grin. He turned slowly in my direction and looked like he wanted to shove me against one of the jeeps and spank me raw.

"Who the *fuck* told you that?" I pointed to him, still smiling, and he deemed me worthy of a rare eye roll. "Right, other me blabbed everything, didn't he? *God damn it.* Get in the jeep and stop looking at me like that."

We walked to the closest jeep and I hauled myself into the driver's seat via the step at foot level because they were so high off the ground. Arthur was talking to the soldier but he stopped when he saw me adjusting the seat for my short torso and long legs.

"You're not fucking driving, move over," he complained loudly enough for the entire airport to hear.

"I used to live at the castle, therefore, I'm driving us there." As Knight hopped in beside me, I leaned over, getting right in Arthur's grumpy face outside of the open door. "Get in the jeep and stop looking at me like that."

Anastasia settled herself in the back along with Olivier and we waited for Arthur to get everyone loaded up before he got into the front seat next to Knight and signaled for us to leave. I started the jeep, rolling out of the airport and onto the narrow country roads of England that were barely big enough for one of the jeeps. If any cars came in the other direction, we'd be screwed, but thankfully we were alone until we reached a city street.

"Other side of the road," Arthur warned when I almost pulled into the wrong lane.

"*Shhhut up*," I murmured, heaving the steering wheel to the side. "I've never driven here before, they didn't have cars last time."

"Do we have to go through here? Alistair could have spies anywhere," Knight worried when we started passing store fronts and apartments full of humans.

"Can't help it, it's the only way to the castle. Once we're closer, we can leave the jeeps and go on foot. Turn here," he said, pointing almost before it was too late. The jeep was so massive, it was difficult to turn, not to mention it felt like the power steering was broken. I was bent in half trying to turn it and Knight put his hand on the wheel to assist until we were turned into the correct lane. "And here."

"Damn it!" We made it to the next turn, and after huffing and straightening myself in the seat, I saw what was at the end of the long road: the vampire castle. It looked pretty much the same as I remembered, massive and imposing, and Estinien had been doing his job of grounds keeper because everything looked pristine.

"*Shit*," Arthur swore, and I saw what had made him swear. Sentries were outside the castle, patrolling the grounds with rifles. We weren't close enough to smell them, but I assumed either they were human or he'd brought back his potion that allowed turned vampires to be in the sunlight. The second seemed more likely since Alistair had little regard for human life. "Go there, to that parking lot." Knight helped me turn again one last time and we parked as the rest of the jeeps came in behind us in the large concrete area, everyone piling out at once and gathering in the center. "Olivier, take someone and go scope out the place. It looks like Alistair has guards outside and we need to know how many." She was off with a burly looking Hunter that had tattoos on his shaved head and they disappeared into a side alley. We were refreshing everyone's knowledge of the floor plan I'd drawn out when they returned.

"I counted at least a hundred on the ground," Olivier huffed, trying to catch her breath. "Arthur, they're not humans. They're turned vampires."

"In the sunlight?" Anastasia asked sharply, the shock echoing around our ranks.

Arthur gave me a look, remembering what I'd said about the potion, and held a hand up for everyone to be quiet. "This makes our job easy. No humans, no issues. They outnumber us, but we'll fight as hard and as long as possible. Get in, find Alistair, and end him. That's our mission." He rolled up the floor plans and tossed them into the jeep. "Move out."

We split up into pre-assigned groups to approach from all sides, and snuck down the city streets, the castle getting closer and closer with each step. The perimeter gate got destroyed under Arthur's fists, letting us all inside the grounds.

It was now or never.

This was why I was brought back, to stop Alistair and protect the future.

I clasped my mates hands in one final gesture before we took off running across the grass, moving as a perfectly matched pack, the way we did in the days when we hunted humans. Knight and Arthur stayed on my sides, my senses pushing out as I ran to reveal the soldiers waiting for us. We hit the first small group and easily took them down, leaving their bodies behind when we continued towards the castle. Stopping for a few more patrols, once the castle was before us, the army Olivier had seen was out in full force and already attacking the rest of our ranks.

We ran full speed, launching ourselves into the fray, pulling vampires off our comrades and slicing our enemies to the ground. Arthur was up in the middle where the biggest group of turned were, and I feinted to the side when one came at Knight, tripping it and slicing it open with one finger for trying to hurt my mate.

Olivier shouted Arthur's name over the roar of battle and I saw him go down. My feet stood frozen for a moment before I ran head first through the ranks, no matter what would happen when I got there, stabbing anything I could see until Arthur was in my sights. Knight was there, helping me pull bodies off Arthur that he'd killed on his way down.

Arthur went still, seeing something above our heads on

one of the castle balconies. "Lisbeth, move!" I barely had time to look up when Knight was there, standing between me and the threat. Something was thrown at us, his body whipped back in a movement that stole the air from my lungs, and he fell down with a lance sticking out of his heart.

His chest deflated with a final breath, and his eyes were vacant with the glassy tell of death.

15

THE NECROMANCER

The scream that came from my throat was so full of agony and rage, the entire battlefield stilled in fear.

I knelt before my lover's body and felt his neck amidst the rising pool of blood, but my ears knew his heart had stopped. Arthur was right beside me, pulling the lance out, and we waited for him to heal, but nothing happened.

We looked up and locked eyes, and no words had to be spoken between us. My mate and I stood as one, fangs and claws out, turning to the battle before us, and we charged in a rage like I'd never felt before. Nothing survived the Hunter and his mate, we tore through every enemy before us with god-like strength, and when they were all dead, without missing a beat we were inside the castle. There were more turned waiting, but they didn't stand a chance against us.

Our army followed behind, more afraid of us than our enemies, until we'd combed through the entire estate and couldn't find our quarry.

"Spread out," I growled out, my fangs and claws bloody. "Check the back field, they might've..." I stopped when my senses picked up a scent I knew well. Estinien. Arthur was on my flank instantly and we followed it outside where a trail led us to the vast land behind the castle that a retreating Alistair and Estinien were running across like cowards. It took little effort to overcome them, launching myself onto Alistair's back while Arthur took out Estinien.

"You killed my mate," Arthur ground out through his fangs, holding Estinien's worthless face to his. "You threw that lance and it killed him."

"I'd do it again, he was a filthy werewolf. You sully our kind by touching him," Estinien challenged, and before he could get another word out, Arthur had swiped his neck open, ending him forever.

The satisfaction was fleeting when I turned my attention back to Alistair, rolling him until he faced me. He was as attractive as the drawings I'd seen of him with his silver hair and chiseled jaw, but I didn't care what he looked like. I wrapped my hand around his worthless neck. "You took my family away. You're the reason they're gone, and I'm never getting them back." Tears of rage escaped my eyes, falling onto his face, smearing the dirt on his cheeks.

"I remember you," he choked out with my fist on his throat. "You were the girl Othello raised. Elisabeth. You abandoned me and the other turned vampires like a coward."

"And you turned your back on us to get your pitiful revenge. But you messed with the wrong girl, and that was your biggest mistake." I squeezed his neck with both hands, his skin tearing and the veins popping, covering me with his blood, then my fingers met in the middle and I ripped my hands out. He went limp, his worthless life finally ended.

I stood on weak legs, my adrenaline waning as reality was coming back. Though my limbs didn't want to move ever again, Arthur met my eyes and we walked back to where Knight's body lay, still motionless and empty. His hand was already turning cold when I picked it up and knelt beside him.

Nothing mattered now. I'd never hold him again. I'd never see my Jason or Gwen again. I should've made him leave. I should've protected him with my life, with everything I had.

Arthur fell to his knees beside me, and for the first time ever in my memory, tears formed in his eyes and he wept aloud for the man we loved, the sobs shaking his body so hard he almost bent in half. It broke me, it shattered me into so many pieces, I knew I would never recover.

When I had no more tears to give, my rage grew again, this time at the very people who did this to me, the ones who took my life away. I was happy, everything was fine, and they fucked it all up. I stood, wiping furiously at my eyes until I could see well enough to rip the necklace off my neck that they'd given me.

"Stand back," I ordered, and my army did so, letting me open the locket front, and the portal to Highborn opened before us. "Mother, help Arthur pick Knight up."

"Lisbeth, he's dead. We should take him home," she said gently.

I pierced her with my deadly glare. "Do as I ask or I swear to god, I will never speak to you again." She rushed over and helped settle Knight's body between her and Arthur, then they walked through the portal with me right behind them, Olivier jumping in before it closed.

Highborn was before us, towering and intimidating, and I hated the sight of it. We walked to the front gate and Isabelle was rushing up to us with her purple dress pulled up to her knees. She stopped cold when she saw us holding a corpse.

"Oh my god, what happened?"

I got between her and my family. "My mate is dead, and your necromancer is going to resurrect him, or I will raze this castle to the ground."

Her timid eyes looked Knight's body over. "But he's a werewolf."

"You'd better hope to god you've got a spell for that then, because I'm not in the mood for mistakes."

Her scent stinking of fear, she sighed and took her wand out, opening the doorway for us. "Alright then, bring him in." She led us up the hill to the courtyard where the children stared at us in horror, especially when they saw my bloodied fangs that hadn't retracted since Knight's death. The little witches scurried away, whispering about how scary we looked.

Isabelle led us through the foyer and up some stairs to a room that looked like a giant supplies closet. Headmaster Cauldron and Selene were there, inspecting the shelves and writing down their inventory. Selene gasped when we walked in.

"Witches brew, what happened?"

I helped Arthur lay Knight's cold body on the floor and glared up at her. "I stopped Alistair like you asked me to, and he killed my mate. You took *everything* from me. You promised I would get my life back." My chin wobbled, my tears falling down my face. "Help me. Bring him back, please. I'll do anything, I'll pay any price. I don't care what it is."

Cauldron's look of pity told me exactly how pathetic I looked. "We'll do everything we can, you have my word. But you need to calm down, your strength is waning and you're expecting. It's not good for the babies."

"Babies?" Arthur asked, but got interrupted when Jaz appeared in the doorway with a tall brown haired boy behind her. He wore a stylish suit with devil-may-care curls, and carried a coffin shaped backpack.

"Holla! Someone ask for a necromancer- ahh gross! Dead person." Her lip curled and her nose scrunched up in disgust.

The boy rolled his eyes at her. "You're a necromancer, you can't think corpses are gross. That's like a baker hating cake."

"Alec, you're a joy. Stand over there and hush." She cracked her knuckles and came to squat beside Knight's body, inspecting him like he was a haunch of meat. "Mmm, he's only been dead for... ten, twenty minutes? That's good. What's his full name?"

Arthur answered for me because I could hardly speak with my fangs starting to hurt. "Jason Knight Trimble."

"Hey, Jason! Get your ass- ahh, there you are." She looked up at an empty space in the room. "Say hi, everyone. Ya boy's here."

"I find this child's skills inadequate," Arthur complained loudly. "Is there a different necromancer? Someone less basic?"

Jaz turned with shock. "You did *not* just call me basic. You're gonna feel real stupid when you find out I'm the only necromancer. Yeah, that's right. It's me or nothing. You feeling dumb yet, cuz I will roast your ass into next night." She flicked her finger, motioning for him to back his ass up. "Anywho, Lisbeth, awesome to see you again. Sorry your boyfriend is dead. That's a bummer. He's saying hi, by the way. He says your ass looks bombin' in that outfit." She looked up and scowled at the air. "I know that's not what you said, but I know you thought it. Bruh, be serious. She's as fly as a plane. Also he says you're pregnant with triplets, don't know how he knows that, but okay. Kinda creepy, using your ghost senses to stare at her uterus. Rude much?"

"That's what I was about to say before Jaz arrived," Cauldron explained. "It seems that the potion we gave you was only intended for witches. When used on a supernatural, it has unintended side effects."

"You're getting a three for one special, hooray!" Jaz called out, waving her hands. "Okay, can we stop talking about babies, I've got a corpse to raise."

"You've raised a corpse before, right?" Arthur asked, still unconvinced.

"Pssh, duuuh! What, you think I'm going to just waltz in here and pretend I know what I'm doing when vampire queen here is covered in blood and about to kill everyone if I don't?" She rolled her eyes, snapped her fingers, and a list appeared in her hand that she handed to Selene. "I need everything on there."

"Does it require a moon phase?" Cauldron asked, helping Selene gather the items from the shelves. "Remember he's a werewolf. They're not like Lycans, they shift with the moon."

Jaz pondered that for a moment, staring at Knight's body this way and that like it held secrets only she could see. "No, it should be fine. If he'd been dead longer, sure, but it's not even been an hour." She snapped her fingers at Alec who had been standing far away until then, and she took a coffin shaped backpack from him when he was close enough. Producing two large pieces of chalk from an inner pocket of the bag, she walked to the center of the room and started marking out a circle with shapes inside and runic lettering, all without using a book. She just seemed to know exactly what to draw.

Isabelle approached, inspecting the work. "You've worked

in his wolf state into the wording, that's very interesting. It will ensure he's brought back in his former state."

Selene and Cauldron finished gathering the supplies as Jaz finished the chalk lines. They brought everything to her and she started placing bowls of herbs in specifics spots along with lit candles in several colors. Done with that, she brought a metal bowl to me.

"Spit in that." I made a face and she waved the bowl up and down in annoyance. "You've swapped DNA with him, you're carrying his child, I need your spit to bind his soul back to his body." Frowning, I spit into the bowl and she took it away, covering it in herbs. "Put him in the circle, be careful not to mess any of the chalk up." Anastasia and Arthur carried Knight's body to the chalk outline, setting him down and stepping back again to stand beside me.

Arthur grasped my hand tightly, and though I had to, needed to, believe this would work, I steeled myself for the possibility Arthur and I would be going home alone. He sensed my thoughts, squeezing my fingers and massaging my knuckles with his thumb.

No matter what, I'll love you enough for both of them.

His thoughts came into my head, and I took a deep, steadying breath, ready for whatever the outcome would be of Jaz's chalk circle and spit covered herbs.

Jaz put the spit bowl on top of Knight's chest, right where the gaping wound in his heart was, and she lit the spit covered herbs on fire. Then she stood next to him and held out her hand, speaking the odd magical words and the power rushed over her, making her pink tipped curls fly around with mystical wind. The words repeated until her fingers moved like she was clasping someone's hand in hers, and she flew to the ground, pressing that hand to Knight's body.

He came awake with a gasp, knocking the bowl from his chest and extinguishing the herb fire. "What in the hell? Where..." He looked up and over at us, and we were on him in a moment, Arthur holding him from one side and me from another. "Oww," he winced from our intense hugs.

Jaz started blowing out the candles, smiling sweetly at our display. "Careful, he's still weak. It'll pass soon."

"You're alive," I breathed, my fangs finally retracting and my rage receding with his warmth beneath me once more. Everything was okay again, everything was as it should be. "I've never felt so alone in my entire life, not even when I thought you were dead before. I wanted to die."

"Ssh," Knight soothed. "I'm back, I'm never leaving again."

"Arthur ugly cried," I sobbed, holding Knight so close my arms hurt.

The stoic warrior did so again at the mention of it, sniffling and crying against Knight's neck. Knight delicately wiped the tears from our lover's cheek and held both of us until we calmed down. As soon as Jaz approved it, we left with the promise to return so Cauldron could check on the babies.

TWO MONTHS PASSED and in-between negotiating more peace treaties with the Lycans and changing the way turned vampires were treated, everything was going well. I went to bed every night snuggled between two of my mates and my growing belly. Every morning I woke up looking for Balthazar, hoping he had returned during the night, but he was still gone.

One day I came back up to our rooms and flopped onto the couch, my belly already full term size with the triplets even though I had more than a few months to go. Arthur was there immediately to rub my feet while Knight brought me a pillow for my lower back. Tired and hurting, I started crying, unable to hold it in any longer. I wanted my Incubus back. I needed him by my side again.

The scent of lavenders arrived a second before Balthazar did, a man standing beside him that looked almost exactly like... me. Balthazar's glow was gone, and his suit looked like it hadn't been washed in decades.

"The Bicus release the immortal being Balthazar to your custody," the other Incubus said, staring right at me as he spoke. "He is no longer welcome in the Bicus realm."

I was up off the couch and crossing the carpet to throw myself into Balthazar's arms before his companion even finished speaking. "Where have you *been*?" I asked him furiously, even though I knew the answer. "I've been worried sick, I thought you were never coming home."

"I'm sorry, my love," he said quietly, smoothing his hand over my hair. "My request was a difficult one. It has taken many years to find the answer." The way he was looking at me, it was the way he looked at our baby after he'd been in the Bicus realm for decades, unable to see her for so long.

"It's been at least a century since Balthazar came, requesting we remove his ability to sire new vampires," the other Incubus answered. I looked from him to Balthazar in horror and held my lover close to me, his arms coming around my back, holding me as tightly as he could with my belly in the way. "There was only one way to remove his virility, and it took us a very long time to discover how, which is why so much time passed in the Bicus realm. In order to comply with his request, we had to strip him of his powers. He's no longer an Incubus, but he said this is what he wanted. He gave it up for you."

The Incubus' words brought me up, looking into his eyes, and with a start I realized they were the same violet color as mine. He knew the instant I made the connection and I met his timid smile with a scowl.

"Piss off," I told him flatly, and he disappeared without a trace. Taking Balthazar's head between my hands, I kissed him deeply for several minutes. "You stupid fool, giving that up for me." Another burning kiss. "Staying in the Bicus realm for one hundred years." Kisses over and over. "You're so stupid."

He rested against my forehead and held me when my tirade was over. "I can't see what you want anymore. I can't see your desires, your needs. It's like being blind."

I kissed him again, my body already warming up under his touch. "Then I'll just tell you."

"I'd like that very much." Leaning against my nose, he breathed in deeply, taking my scent in with every expanse of his lungs. "I missed you *so much*." His voice broke with the words and he reached a hand up to clutch my hair. "There were days when I lost hope that I would ever see you again. I pictured you here alone and my heart ached so much, I wanted to rip it from my chest. I have never felt such heartache, not in all my time on the earth." The hand in my hair trembled so badly he was forced to drop it, and he dipped his chin to kiss me, tears mixing with our lips until there was so much moisture I had to tip my head back and wipe it all away with my sleeve. I'd never seen him cry so much, not ever.

"What are you now? You're not an Incubus anymore." I kissed him again, through all the tears.

"I'm simply an immortal, like Clara is. Not fragile, just plain and boring. I used to bring women to their knees with just one look, and now I'll have to settle for actual skill."

I laughed, puffing out more tears between us. "You have plenty of that, and I don't find you plain and boring at all, even if you're simply immortal now."

He looked up at Knight and Arthur standing nearby. "There are some advantages to my new state, however. Something I've been thinking about doing since I left, and now I can." Before he explained what he meant, he left my arms and went right up to Arthur, kissing my vampire lover on the lips with a longing that brought my warmth to a raging inferno. Then he kissed Knight, holding the werewolf flush against his lower half and drawing a moan from Knight's lips.

I inhaled sharply, trying to contain my excitement, and it drew them apart, both staring over at me with mischievous grins.

"Don't just stand there," Balthazar challenged. "I can't introduce myself to your lovers without you." I happily walked with them to our bedroom where we reacquainted ourselves with Balthazar for hours until we fell asleep entwined, and everything was right again.

16

EPILOGUE

*L*ace and flowers reigned today.

I dressed my baby Gwen up in her pink dress and kissed her before holding her against my shoulder. She settled in the crook of my neck, one of her tiny hands pressed to me. Her dark black hair was already curling at the tips though she was still twenty-one hours old, and she had the deep tanned skin of her father, Knight.

"Ready?" Arthur asked me, holding the small bag with Gwen's diapers inside. I nodded and he kissed me on the lips before we left the farm house. Waiting outside was our family, all smiles amidst the flowers and food we'd set out.

The triplets, Kitty, Jason, and Dreya, arrived a month early, and though they'd come all at once this time, they were the same precious babies I'd had before. Kitty still had Balthazar's blue mixed with my purple in her eyes. Jason still had

Knight's deep brown eyes, and his sense of humor. Dreya's beautiful blonde hair looked just like Arthur's. While only five years in age, the triplets had grown to adults already, something Headmaster Cauldron attributed to the potion's abnormal effect on me. As jarring as it was, we suspected the same would happen to Gwen, so I was enjoying her tiny state as much as possible. I'd been robbed of her childhood before, I wouldn't miss a moment of it this time.

Lucas held his bride Clara to him with Anastasia nearby, Olivier stood with Renard, who had decided to become a vampire again and pledge his love to the woman he'd given his heart to since the first moment they met. Merrick was there too and her opinion of me was much warmer this time around, and beside her was the gangly Dom who was making moony eyes at Kitty. Cameron, still decidedly human despite his growing affection for Merrick, was next to Galen, my other former companion.

And Knight stood at the end of the line with Balthazar, holding hands and waiting for us to approach with our tiny daughter. Arthur walked me down until we joined our mates, kissing each in turn. I turned and presented Gwen to our family, and they cooed over her, telling me how beautiful she was.

We ate cake, we partied hard, and we put the baby to bed early.

The triplets left to visit their friends while the rest of our family went home, leaving me and my three mates on the front porch, sitting together on our large wicker couch.

Leaning into Knight's embrace with Arthur on my other side and Balthazar's hand in mine, I stared off into the world I saved. Though it costed me everything, I refused to accept the loss of my family, and I'd regained all that was taken from me. And I would do it again, for no other reason than to have my lovers by my side and my children in my arms.

"You think we'll ever have to save the world again," I mused, rubbing my hand against Arthur's leg.

"God, I hope not," Knight answered firmly, leaning to kiss my forehead. "We've got the kids now, they can save the world. I'm too lazy for that shit. Plus, I've got everything I'll ever need right here."

As did I.

NOTES

3. HIGHBORN

1. Balzjanyóur nappnia lanliápob: I greatly desire you (Balthazar) by my side.

Glossary

*B*icus: A collective term for the sibling creatures known as Incubus and Succubus.

Bonding ceremony: A vampire wedding involving a vow between the couple, exchanging of each other's blood, and mixing their blood together through a cut on their wrists.

Born vampires: The product of an Incubus and human female union. They can turn humans, create drones, and give birth to new vampires. Born vampires must drink fresh human blood every day. Drinking bagged human blood cannot sustain them and will cause them to slowly starve.

Companion: A term for the humans that serve vampires. They sign a ten year contract and are chosen by a vampire to live in their rooms, and be willingly bitten once a day to feed the vampire. Once their contract is up they can either renew it, or they can leave with a promised sum of money upon contract termination.

Council: A group comprised of the heads of each vampire Order. They oversee all vampires, pass judgement for infractions, and direct the vampire Hunters.

Dhampir: The product of a vampire and human union. None were known to exist as the two species typically do not mix romantically.

Frenzy: A state vampires reach when they are so starved of blood their body can no longer cope. They become wild, their eyes glow red, and they will attack until their hunger is sated.

Hunters: A group comprised solely of Born vampires whose sole purpose is to hunt down any vampire that has broken the law, and either bring them to justice or execute them.

Incubus: A creature of seduction, built for the sole purpose of coupling with female humans to create new Born vampires. If an Incubus falls in love, they develop a distinctive scent.

Lycans: The product of a Primal werewolf and human female union. They can shift into a wolf whenever they like.

Primal werewolves: Originally human men who have been scratched by a succubus, turning them to a werewolf when the full moon rises.

The Bicus plane: A mystical realm only accessible to those with the blood of the Bicus. Time moves differently inside the plane, moving slower or faster than Earth depending on the moment.

The Order Acilino: Location in Spain, name translates to "Eagle."

The Order Bête: Location in Canada, name translates to "Beast."

The Order Dedliwan: Location in Australia, name translates to "Deadly."

The Order Engel: Location in Greenland, name translates to "Angel."

The Order Gennadi: Location in Russia, name translates to "Noble."

The Order Janiccat: Location in Malaysia, name translates to "Born."

The Order Khalid: Location in Algeria, name translates to "Immortal."

The Order Oleander: Location in the United States, name translates to "Poisonous."

The Order Qiángdù: Location in China, name translates to "Strength."

The Order Raposa: Location in Brazil, name translates to "Fox."

The Order Safed: Location in India, name translates to "Undamaged."

The Order Sangre: Location in Mexico, name translates to "Blood."

The turned vampires: Vampires that used to be humans and have been. Note: the word "turned" in reference to this type of vampire is never capitalized, hence referring to them as "the turned" to avoid this. They cannot turn humans, or give birth. The turned must drink human blood every day. Unlike the Born vampires, the turned vampires can survive on bagged blood.

Vaewolf: The product of a Primal werewolf or Lycan and a vampire union. They can shift into a wolf whenever they like, they have vampire fangs, and they require blood to heal if they are seriously injured. They do not require daily blood like vampires do.

Vipyre: The product of an Incubus and vampire female union. An incredibly rare creature, only one has ever been known to exist, but it is most likely due to lost knowledge as these creatures have been written about in Incubi lore.

Bathory Family

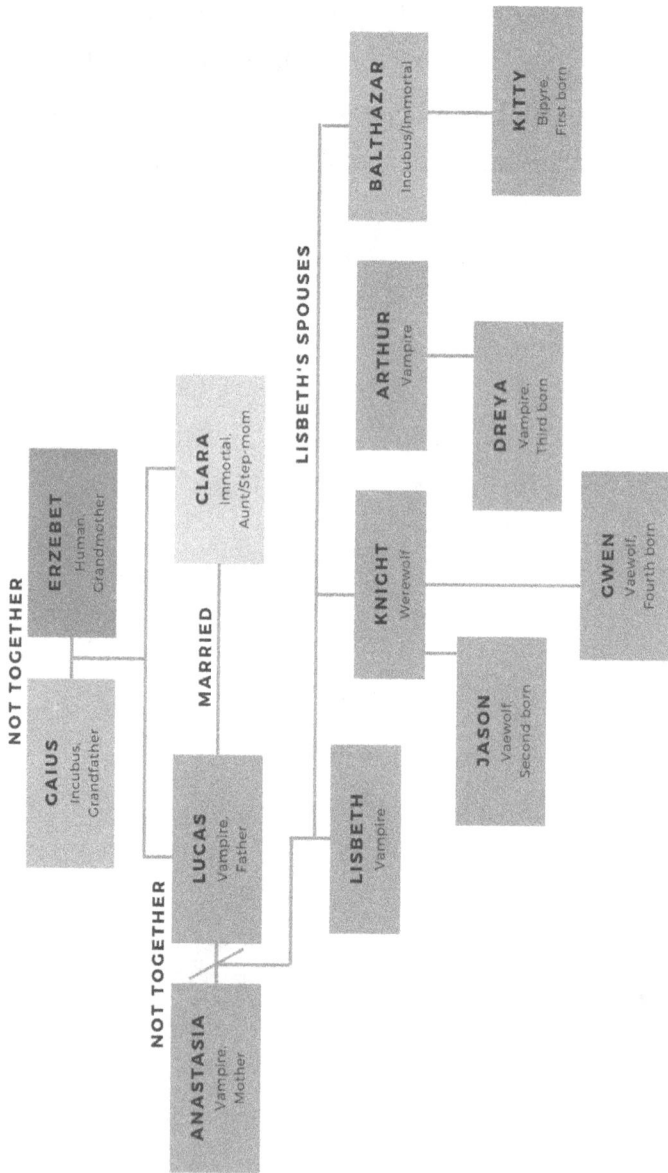

NOT TOGETHER

GAIUS
Incubus,
Grandfather

ERZEBET
Human,
Grandmother

CLARA
Immortal,
Aunt/Step-mom

MARRIED

LUCAS
Vampire,
Father

NOT TOGETHER

ANASTASIA
Vampire,
Mother

LISBETH
Vampire

LISBETH'S SPOUSES

KNIGHT
Werewolf

ARTHUR
Vampire

BALTHAZAR
Incubus/Immortal

JASON
Vaewolf,
Second born

KNIGHT
Werewolf

GWEN
Vaewolf,
Fourth born

DREYA
Vampire,
Third born

KITTY
Bipyre,
First born

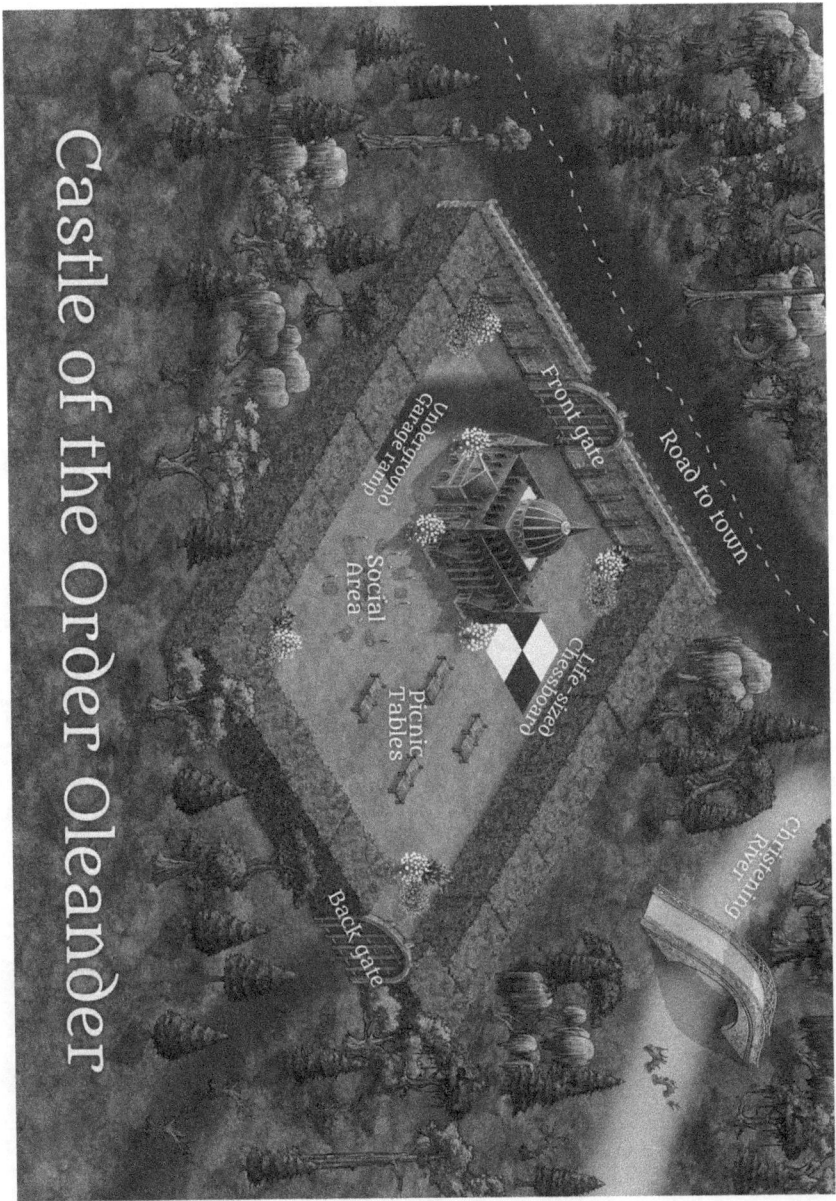

Castle of the Order Oleander

Road to Town

Front gate

Underground Garage ramp

Social Area

Life-sized Chessboard

Picnic Tables

Back gate

Christening River

ABOUT THE AUTHOR

Photo by Elizabeth Dunlap

Elizabeth Dunlap is the author of several fantasy books, including the Born Vampire series. She's never wanted to be anything else in her life, except maybe a vampire. She lives in Texas with her boyfriend, their daughter, and a very sleepy chihuahua named Deyna.

You can find her online at
www.elizabethdunlap.com

facebook.com/elizabethdunlapnifty
twitter.com/edunlapnifty
instagram.com/edunlapnifty
goodreads.com/Elizabeth_Dunlap
bookbub.com/authors/elizabeth-dunlap
amazon.com/author/ElizabethDunlap

CPSIA information can be obtained
at www.ICGtesting.com
Printed in the USA
LVHW092106231120
672493LV00021B/137

9 781393 052784